FIRST
WIVES CLUB
COAST SALISH STYLE

THEYTUS BOOKS

Library and Archives Canada Cataloguing in Publication

Maracle, Lee, 1950-
First wives club : Coast Salish style / by Lee Maracle.

ISBN 978-1-894778-95-4

1. Coast Salish Indians--Fiction. I. Title.

PS8576.A6175F57 2010   C813'.54   C2010-901345-X

Printed in Canada by Gauvin Press

www.theytus.com
In Canada: Theytus Books, Green Mountain Rd., Lot 45, RR#2, Site 50, Comp. 8
Penticton, BC, V2A 6J7, Tel: 250-493-7181
In the USA: Theytus Books, P.O. Box 2890, Oroville, Washington, 98844

Patrimoine   Canadian
canadien   Heritage

Canada Council   Conseil des Arts
for the Arts   du Canada

BRITISH COLUMBIA
ARTS COUNCIL
Supported by the Province of British Columbia

Theytus Books acknowledges the support of the following:
We acknowledge the financial support of the Government of Canada through the
Canada Book Fund for our publishing activities. We acknowledge the support of
the Canada Council for the Arts which last year invested $20.1 million in writing
and publishing throughout Canada. Nous remercions de son soutien le Conseil des
Arts du Canada, qui a investi 20,1 millions de dollars l'an dernier dans les lettres
et l'édition à travers le Canada. We acknowledge the support of the Province of
British Columbia through the British Columbia Arts Council.

First Wives Club:
Coast Salish Style

Lee Maracle

Contents

First Wives Club:
Coast Salish Style

There is an old saying: "The older you get, the less sex you have and the more you talk about it." That makes older people oral experts on sex (pardon the pun) when it is a little late to be considered sexy. Today's society is focused on *imaging* sexiness only through youth, but many of our Elders don't buy into that and, of course, neither do I.

Falling in love and being sexy are not always tied together. But for sure, falling in love inspires us to fall back to the sexy machinations of our youth. As long as sexual desire burns inside, we remain sexy and consequently forever young. I had an opportunity to witness one of my Elders fall in love in her sixties and it struck me how much romance became her. Sexy seems to have more to do with desire and aliveness than anything else.

Every now and then my son phones to tell me he is reading some article or other about sex, which is a good thing for a young Salish man to be doing, as you will see later on from the story. He called me some time back to say that sex burns calories and, if the scientists he was quoting were correct, it burns calories at the rate of 3,500 a romp. He added that it was purported to clear the skin of unsightly blemishes and to some degree clear the mind. As such, I am wondering why more of us don't just give up our treadmills, track shoes, skin potions and brain vitamins to opt for a daily romp. On another occasion, he called to tell me that sex is a powerful source of energy and further that it is a source of energy that can only be replenished by consuming it.

I replied, "Too bad."

"Too bad?" he asked.

"Yeah," I answered. "I just can't picture anyone giving an engineer permission to figure out a way to harness that energy—which is too bad, such a waste."

My son says he heard that, despite all of the above, the average person in Canada has sex only once a week (not quite sure how this estimate was arrived at). I imagine Canadians using billions of tons of skin products annually, to little avail, and then swallowing a bunch of vitamins before they run off to public and private gyms, spas, fat farms, etc., all of which are becoming more numerous year to year as the baby boomers acquire that old middle-age spread . . . and I sigh. Makes you wonder.

First Nations people, particularly fifty-five-plus women, are not billed as sexy anywhere by anyone; generally, coupling (pardon the pun) First Nations women with sex is done crudely, when it is done at all. There are no First Nations supermodels or sex icons out there, and procreative sex is spoken about without fanfare. There's also a certain measure of disregard for the femininity and the beauty of the women being referenced.

Don Burnstick is a comic; he looks funny, and he has funny looks, so when he says "I saw a beautiful Ojibway woman, once" and makes a face, people laugh. When he follows that with "It could happen," only half the audience laughs because for some of us this is not all that funny. Underneath his joke is the disqualification of the sexiness of an entire nation of women. Salish humorists try very hard to poke fun at human folly without completely disqualifying humanity itself. We try to have fun with each other and not at each other's expense.

Western society's values have always confused me. On the one hand, sexiness in young women is desired. On the other hand, a woman actually engaging in sex has been considered immoral for a long time.

"What good does it do to cajole and persuade a woman into having sex with you, then humiliate and berate her for it when she gives in?" an old chief asked some white guy a couple hundred years ago. It seems that while women are burdened with the responsibility of looking sexy, permission to engage in sex is a male prerogative, though that is changing slowly. Good for me. As I age, the burden of carrying a bad reputation weighs and fatigues. "You've come a long way, baby" was an ad for a very long time, and most women got the reference. But the pun is, of course, the business of "coming," and in the sexual department it is the men who have been doing the coming a long way baby.

So, what is sexy? I have to say that the act itself seems hilarious to me when I am not engaged in it. There is nothing we do that is so much fun but looks so ridiculous in the doing—two people fumbling and rolling around, then bouncing up and down on each other, all the while uttering odd grunts and sighs. The prelude to sexual intercourse, though, is lovely. When sexual desire is sparked, no matter how old we are, our movements become elegant and smooth, determined, nearly urgent and sure. Our voices acquire that husky come-hither musicality that is so sweet. We feel our curves; our chests/breasts push themselves out almost with a will of their own. Our hips sway and our nipples perk up and become sensitive. We can feel the desire rising from our loins. Our skin tingles. Whatever stress and worries we have on our minds slip away for the moment. We lean into the conversation of a prospective lover, soften our voices, twirl our fingers in our hair, bat our eyes. We giggle and laugh at jokes we wouldn't normally consider funny. We reach out and sneak little touches, extend quick and secretive caresses in those forbidden places, move into our significant other, brushing nipples against their arm or their chest in feigned innocence, as though it were an accident. We imbue the world around us with sexual meaning, which gives birth to some good old sexually laden double entendre.

"Coffee?" He purrs, glancing sideways, eyes intense with desire and full of some crazy kind of knowing where this is leading.

"Oh, yeah," I answer, lips swelling, thighs quivering; my mouth relaxes and pouts. I am careful not to completely close it. I am doubly careful to hold the pout. My tongue plays an old game of sneak-up with my barely open mouth. He looks at me with lascivious intent, sucks in his breath and holds. Oh yeah, this is where I want it to go.

"Sugar?" He drawls as though he considered it my very essence, my name.

"Yesss." I am very near to orgasm. This is where I want to be.

In the western world, men are expected to court women. In the Salish world, the adoption of this courtship tradition is in its infancy. In the original Salish cultures, it was the women who chose the partners and our women Elders who negotiated the marriage—if there was even going to be one. If a woman desired a man and no marriage was in the offing for her, there was going to be an affair of the heart, because women were free to indulge in sexual activity if and when they pleased. Unlike some other First Nation cultures, sex and morality were not that tightly connected (again, pardon the pun).

As a young person, I was asked by my chiefs to organize the youth and encourage them to attend the first All-Chiefs conference in Kamloops, B.C. So I called a Youth Gathering to be held at the local Indian Friendship Centre in Vancouver, notified all the young people I knew and made a presentation on behalf of the not quite fully formed Union of B.C. Indian Chiefs. It was 1968, the year the skimpy, sexy T-shirt came on the scene for young women. I was wearing one, along with a pretty snug pair of jeans—and no bra. (It was the sixties.) An Elder from Saskatchewan named Ernest Tootoosis came up after my talk and complimented my speech. After a pregnant pause he added, staring at my cleavage (small though it was), "But maybe you should dress more traditional," and he pointed at my shirt. I knew what he meant; he was well known for scolding women for wearing sexy clothing.

"Real Indian women wore long dresses covering their legs and buttoned to the neck," I wanted to say. Just in front of me was a picture of a group of First Nations men holding old rifles and sporting little mini-skirts atop their Western pants and shirts. Should I tell him that I'll wear a long dress buttoned to the neck if he wears a mini-skirt, like in the picture? He probably wouldn't get it.

"You're right," I replied instead, and pulled a sweater over my T-shirt.

Cree women apparently wore long deerskin dresses before Europeans arrived and traditionally covered their bodies pretty much head to toe. But what Tootoosis did not know was that, prior to the arrival of the good Oblates, Salish women did not wear shirts during the summer or at a good old bone game. (It really is called a bone game.)

In this era of Aboriginal Studies, there is the tendency to *brown wash* or clean up our past before passing on our traditions. And sometimes it gets cleaned up in accordance with someone else's current morality. I am not advocating a return to the old Lahal games practices, in which women sang and danced half-naked, enthusiastically cupping and bouncing their beautiful breasts in an attempt to distract the other team, but we should know a little about who we are before we become someone else's idea of who we should be. Sex is so central to adult human interaction, whether it is hetero or homo, that every adult at some point feels their loins fire up with desire. Sexiness is our response. Sexual permission, however, is structured by the social milieu from which we arise.

A fellow Wolf Clan woman from Six Nations told me she was going to visit my home. She is like many Six Nations women: sexy, tall and with one of those lyrical, husky and luscious voices we all love to listen to. Salish people, in general, do not reach the average height of Mohawks.

"So, you are going to have fun with my little people," I said, adding that we were the "cutest people in the world."

She did. She returned and said that everyone there was short, thin and, exactly like I had said, cute. Even the men, she added with a delicious laugh. She said they were so cute and so small; she wanted to put a couple of them in her coat pocket and take them home.

"The men would just come up to me and look at me smiling. It was so funny, so odd. What was that all about?" she asked.

"They were making a pass," I said. "The smile is telling you, 'I'm available and willing.'"

"You mean all I had to do was grab one of them and take them home?"

"Pretty much," I said.

"No wonder West Coast women are so aggressive," she added.

Which brings me to the story and the teachings I acquired before my body opened itself up to sexual desire. Our stories are told in sections. This section is used to teach women to use "weasel medicine" to manipulate men to do the right thing by their families. It also teaches us the power of women, their desire and their sexiness. It also grants sexual permission to women to engage their sexuality in a way that they see fit.

It was after the flood, the tidewaters were receding. The earth had cleaned up much of the cadaverous mess that occurred after the loss of so much mammalian life. Our response to the flood was not as tidy as the Christian one. First, God did not pay us a visit to warn us beforehand that it was coming, although the creator visited some of us to tell us where to find safe places while we were thrashing about in the midst of the resulting tsunami. This story might have turned out differently if God had given us either the time or instructions to build an ark and climb aboard with all the paired animals.

When the flood hit us, most of us perished. Those women who survived made it to the tops of some very large mountains with help from one sister or another. The heroes in most of our flood stories are women—sisters who saved Elders, other sisters, their children, or sacrificed themselves for expectant mothers and the like. The women did not generally rescue men. At least, if any woman did rescue a man, that story did not get handed down in my family. I am not sure if this is true but my mother and grandmother used to say that women did not try to save the men because they couldn't save both men and women and while it takes all the women to re-populate a village, it takes only one man.

As the waters receded, one such pair of sisters, one of whom had rescued the other, climbed down from the mountain on which they had waited out the flood. Only one sister had a child with her, the other had no children. They were determined to make a go of it on the valley floor at the ocean's edge. They constructed a lean-to from woven cedar mats and began life anew. One day, one of the women was washing out the mats at the river's mouth, where the ocean meets the shore, when she spotted a canoe. It wasn't a big canoe. Inside it was a solitary man. There he was standing in the canoe looking toward her. Behind him the sun dappled diamond glints of light; as it fell behind the sea, it reddened the sky and silhouetted his perfect body. Her legs quivered and her lips swelled. Oh yes, he was yummy, so pretty he hurt to look at.

She decided she would have him. Now Salish women know how to capture a man. She turned her back on him and began singing an old love song. She leaned forward, butt sticking out, and rotated her hips, swaying them to the music of her song. Salish women know that Salish men love that little bumblebee dance of the hips. Sure enough he paddled ashore. As he arrived, she turned her face toward him slightly, just enough so he could see the fire of desire in her eyes, but she kept singing and swaying and of course washing her mats. Humans are funny. We don't want to seem too obvious, so we pretend to be doing something, anything but seduc-ing the person we are seducing, while we leer, we geek and poke out our butts, our breasts, bat our eyes and just generally do anything we can to get laid.

He landed, tied up his canoe and followed her to her lean-to. They got busy. He stayed all winter. The child that was with the women nagged him. He became increasingly annoyed, and as he became annoyed, he grew restless for the sea. Spring rolled around, and so he hopped into his canoe and hit the sea waves. Meanwhile, both joy and tragedy struck the sisters. They were running out of food. Because one of them was now pregnant, the other gave up her share of food to feed her pregnant sister and the young child. Sacrificing for her sister, the child and the baby on the way, she did not survive.

The surviving sister bore her baby and was now alone with her two children (both by different fathers. I see a pattern developing here). While her sister was alive she had been sure the man would return; now that she was alone with small children, she was occasionally plagued with doubt. The loss of her sister meant the loss of her assistance and the winter became increasingly difficult and fraught with hardship. Still, she and the children survived.

The weather began to change in the spring and sure enough, he returned. She was digging for clams and saw him approach. Excited and relieved she started to sing again, turned her back and pushed up those hips he loved so much, and she swayed back and forth to the rhythm of her song. He parked his canoe. On her back was this baby, but he didn't know what it was.

He asked her, "What's that ugly thing on your back?"

"You don't know?" she purred, and she trotted her fingers along his arm, his chest and touched his face. The pull of her husky voice distracted his mind and woke up his other head. She picked up her basket of clams and headed for shore. She moved elegantly, slowly and rhythmically, her hips swaying, the light catching them in a magical way as she waltzed her way along the sun-dappled trail. He followed her, focused on those hips and his own desire. Soon he forgot his question. All summer long he complained about the noisy ugly thing, but she never said anything to him when he did. Let him complain, she thought, I know how to quiet him. And she would trail her fingers across his chest and imagine the stories of his journey through the flood for him, telling him how brave and strong he was in her husky come-hither voice. When she did, his mouth dried, his legs quivered and invariably he would end up in her lean-to, forgetting about his complaints. Eventually he grew restless again, though. As he was getting ready to leave that next fall, he asked her again, "Where did you get that thing?"

"You don't know?" she answered.

"No," he said.

"You will know when you need to know," she responded coyly, then lifted her lashes and turned her face partially toward him in that shy way that excited him. This flustered him a little, as she knew it would, and again he forgot what he had asked. He retreated to his canoe still watching her doing that little bumblebee dance with her hips as she swayed back down the trail, the sunlight bouncing first off this hip, then off the other hip. It excited him so to watch her make her way back to her lean-to. He wasn't sure he wanted to leave. He left only after deciding he would always return. She smiled to herself, took one last glance and murmured, "He's coming back for more."

He had spent all summer at her camp. While he was there she had him fix her up an adze and clear the old dead logs that littered the small delta prairie. When he was done, she had him split shakes from the short thick cedar logs and shave the thinner long ones free of their bark. She was making plans for his return.

The next spring, he returned just a little earlier than before. In fact, winter was barely over when he came back. This time, she had another child on her back. Again, he asked her where she got that ugly thing. And again, she lifted her lashes, traced her fingers along his arms and pressed her breasts against his chest and asked if he wasn't just a little tired. "I'm not that tired," he answered with more enthusiasm than he intended. As she pressed her leg up against him, she could feel the swell of his manhood. The question receded.

He worked with even more vigour this time, clearing the delta of old deadwood and making tools for her. Over the winter, the woman had built a weir from the thin long branches he had cut for her the previous summer; she had staked the river and trapped a lot of fish. Now she was busy smoking them. She offered him a bite. They were tasty. The food was getting better, the young man thought, and he noticed that it was also much more plentiful than the first time he had come. He was less inclined to wander. But the first baby was now walking and he often had a snotty nose, which annoyed the man. The little thing was also demanding much of the woman's time. The oldest child also remained bothersome and annoying to the man. Eventually the man grew impatient, and again he determined to leave, though this time it was early winter by the time he dragged himself away.

From the mountaintops, other women who had survived the flood saw the smoke of the woman's fire and noticed that the clearing had increased in size. They decided to leave the mountains and see how this woman managed to clear so much land so quickly. When they arrived at her camp, she invited them to join her and her children. Together they realized they could create a village of survivors. One of the newcomers had a child, so the first woman's children now had a playmate. It was good to have so much company, but the lean-to was not sufficient to protect so many women from the rain. They did their best to build a bigger lean-to, but it was still pretty crowded. The rain fell cold and damp, and the wind chilled them mercilessly. Not only that, but there were several young women without children. They mentioned this to the first woman, who was by now very obviously pregnant again.

"How did you manage to get pregnant?" one asked. "There doesn't seem to be any man around."

"I have a man," she said slyly. "He is off wandering, but he'll be back." And she dipped her hips and let out a sexy growl. They laughed.

"How does that help us?"

"When the weather warms and the tide changes, take the mats to where the ocean meets the river and wash them. If you sing, and your behind does that little bumblebee dance when he comes, he will give you a child."

The older women laughed.

"But he is already attached to you, what chance do I have?" one of the younger ones sighed.

"Just sing and do that little bumblebee thing and he won't be able to resist. He doesn't like children, but it doesn't matter because he doesn't know where babies come from," she told them. "Don't tell him."

"Why?"

"The babies annoy him." The other women found this completely amusing.

Then it happened just as she had said. The man came and saw the second woman on the shore, heard her song, saw her hips dip and sway. He was smitten. After she had her way, he saw the first woman with another new child and asked where she got that thing. As before, the woman laughed and traced her fingers along his arms, dipped and swung her hips, pressed her breasts against his chest and again he forgot his question. He was smitten with First Woman, still. He definitely did not wish to leave. The two women did not mind that he cherished both of them, and they shared his manhood willingly. It was almost too good to be true.

The woman did not mind because with him in camp and the extra women, they were able to go up river and dry their precious *shtwehen*, gather a wider variety of sweet berries, till the camas fields, dry and smoke clams, gather and dry seaweed and other sea vegetables. As they worked, they sang and danced, told stories of the flood and how they survived. Their laughter at the antics of their growing children, the attention and industry of the man all brought joy to the camp. He worked hard, falling trees, splitting shakes for them. But finally, the children began nagging him and annoying him—and he still didn't know how these women got them. So in early winter he left again. This time all the women gathered at the shore to see him off. As they receded toward the clearing, they all sang and swayed their lush hips. The dipping and swaying of all those women pulled and aroused his manhood; the man hesitated, then he saw the children scampering toward the women and he left.

He returned as soon as winter was over. The women were at the edge of the river's mouth. This time they all sang and danced and enticed him to shore. He grew so excited he nearly capsized his canoe. Before they retreated to the lean-to, the first woman told him that they needed a home because their lean-to had almost toppled in a storm; he agreed to build another lean-to. They gave him a lusty look and purred, "Not a lean-to, a dry and warm home, a big home, a long house." As they trailed their fingers along his arms, down his back, across his thighs and pressed their breasts and hips against his chest, his legs, his back, they cajoled him into agreeing to build a Longhouse. It didn't take long before he agreed.

As soon as they had his promise, they retreated one at a time to the lean-to with him. He managed to satisfy the first two but was exhausted by the time the last woman entered the lean-to. He could not arouse himself. He felt so guilty, but the last woman cooed, "That's okay: you have good hands, long thick fingers." He wasn't sure what to do, but the woman seemed to know, and soon she, too, was satisfied. She wasn't worried; he wasn't going anywhere for a while and she would have her chance to become pregnant.

He saw the new babies and again asked where they got them. The women giggled, touched his thigh, his chest and his arms and said, "You don't know?" They all purred.

To this day, no Salish woman has ever broken the promise they made to each other. I know, because every time I told my Salish husband I was pregnant he responded with shock: "How did that happen?" And like all good Salish women before me, I just said, "You don't know?" And I traced my fingers along his arms, his chest and his thighs—and just smiled.

Goodbye Snauq

Raven has never left this place, but sometimes it feels like she has been negligent, maybe even a little dense. Raven shaped us; we are built for transformation. Our stories prepare us for it. Find freedom in the context you inherit; every context is different; discover consequences and change from within, that is the challenge. Still, there is horror in having had change foisted upon you from outside. Raven did not prepare us for what has happened over the past 150 years. She must have fallen asleep some time around the first smallpox epidemic when the T'sleil Waututh Nation nearly perished, and I am not sure she ever woke up.

The halls of this educational institution are empty. The bright white fluorescent bulbs that dot the ceiling are hidden behind great long light fixtures dimming its length. Not unlike the dimness of a Longhouse, but it doesn't feel the same. The dimness of the hallway isn't brightened by a fire in the centre nor warmed by the smell of cedar all around you. There are no electric lights in the Longhouse, and so the dimness is natural. The presence of lights coupled with dimness makes this place seem eerie. I trudge down the dim hallway; my small hands clutch a bright white envelope. Generally, letters from the Government of Canada, in right of the Queen, are threateningly ensconced in brown envelopes; this is from a new government—my own government: the Squamish First Nation. Its colour is an irony. I received it yesterday, broke into a sweat and into a bottle of white wine within five minutes of its receipt. It didn't help. I already knew the contents, even before Canada Post managed to deliver it; Canadian mail is notoriously slow. The television and radio stations were so rife with the news that there was no doubt in my mind that this was my government's official letter informing me that "a deal had been brokered." The Squamish Nation had won the Snauq lawsuit and surrendered any further claim for a fee. The numbers are staggering—$92 million. That is more than triple our total GNP, wages and businesses combined.

As I lay in my wine-soaked state, I thought about the future of the Squamish Nation—development dollars, cultural dollars, maybe even language dollars, healing dollars. I have no right to feel this depressed, to want to be this intoxicated, to want to remove myself from this decision, this moment or this world. I have no right to want to curse the century in which I was born, the political times in which I live, and certainly I have no right to hate the decision makers, my elected officials, for having brokered the deal. In fact, until we vote on it, until we ratify it, it is a deal in theory only. While the wine sloshed its way through my veins to the blood in my brain, pictures of Snauq rolled about. Snauq is now called False Creek. When the Squamish first moved there to be closer to the colonial centre, the water was deeper and stretched from the sea to what is now Clark Drive in the east; it covered the area from Second Avenue in the south to just below Dunsmuir in the north. There was a sandbar in the middle of it, hence the name Snauq. I lay on my couch, Russell Wallace's music CD, *Tso'kam*, blaring in the background—Christ our songs are sad, even the happy ones. Tears rolled down my face. I join the ranks of ancestors I try not to think about—wine-soaked and howling out old Hank Williams crying songs, laughing in between, tears sloshing across the laughter lines—that was the fifties.

My Ta'ah intervenes. Eyes narrowed, she ends the party, clears out the house sending home all those who had a little too much to drink. She confiscates keys from those who are drunk, making sure only the sober drive the block to the reserve. "None of my children are going to get pinched and end up in *hoosegow*."

Addled with the memory, my brain pulls up another drunken soiree, maybe the first one. A group of men gathers around a whiskey keg; their children raped by settlers, they drink until they perish. It was our first run at suicide, and I wonder what inspired their descendents to want to participate in the new society in any way shape or form.

"Find freedom in the context you inherit." From the shadows, Khahtsahlano emerges, eyes dead blind and yet still twinkling, calling out, "Sweetheart, they were so hungry, so thirsty that they drank up almost the whole of Snauq with their dredging machines. They built mills at Yaletown and piled up garbage at the edges of our old supermarket—Snauq. False Creek was so dirty that eventually even the white man became concerned." I have seen archival pictures of it. They dumped barrels of toxic chemical waste from sawmills, food waste from restaurants, taverns and teahouses; thousands of metric tons of human sewage joins the other waste daily. I am drunk, drunk enough to apologize for my nation. So much good can come of this, so why the need for wine to stem the rage?

"The magic of the white man is that he can change everything, everywhere. He even changed the food we eat." Khahtsahlano faces False Creek from the edge of Burrard Inlet holding his white cane delicately in his hand as he speaks to me. The inlet was almost a mile across at that time, but the dredging and draining of the water shrank it. Even after he died in 1967, the dredging and altering of our homeland was not over. The shoreline is gone, in its place are industries squatting where the sea once was. Lonsdale Quay juts out onto the tide and elsewhere, cemented and land-filled structures occupy the inlet. The sea asparagus that grew in the sand along the shore is gone. There is no more of the camas we once ate. All the berries, medicines and wild foods are gone. "The *womans* took care of the food," he says. And now we go to schools like this one and then go to work in other schools, businesses, in Band offices or anyplace that we can, so we can purchase food in modern supermarkets. Khahtsahlano is about to say something else. "Go away," I holler at his picture and suddenly I am sober.

Snauq is in Musqueam territory across the inlet from T'sleil Waututh, but the Squamish were the only ones to occupy it year round, some say as early as 1821, others 1824, still others peg the date as somewhere around the 1850s. Before that, it was a common garden shared by all the friendly tribes in the area. The fish swam there, taking a breather from their ocean playgrounds, ducks gathered, women cultivated camas fields and berries abounded. On the sand bar, Musqueam, T'sleil Waututh and Squamish women till oyster and clam beds to encourage reproduction. Wild cabbage, mushrooms and other plants were tilled and hoed as well. Summer after summer the nations gathered to harvest, likely to plan marriages, play a few rounds of that old gambling game Lahal. Not long after the first smallpox epidemic all but decimated the T'sleil Waututh people, the Squamish people came down from their river homes where the snow fell deep all winter to establish a permanent home at False Creek. Chief George —Chipkayim— built the big Longhouse. Khahtsahlano was a young man then. His son, Khahtsahlano, was born there. Khahtsahlano grew up and married Swanamia there. Their children were born there.

"Only three duffel's worth," the barge skipper is shouting at the villagers. Swanamia does her best to choke back the tears, fingering each garment, weighing its value, remembering the use of each and choosing which one to bring and which to leave. Each spoon, handles lovingly carved by Khahtsahlano, each bowl, basket and bent box must be evaluated for size and affection. Each one requires a decision. Her mind watches her husband's hand sharpening his adze, carving the tops of each piece of cutlery, every bowl and box. She remembers gathering cedar roots, pounding them for hours and weaving each basket. Then she decides: Fill as many baskets as the duffels can hold and leave the rest.

Swanamia faces Burrard Inlet, she cannot bear to look back. Her son winces. Khahtsahlano sits straight up. Several of the women suppress a gasp as they look back to see Snauq's Longhouses on fire. The men who set the fires are cheering. Plumes of smoke affirm that the settlers who keep coming in droves have crowded the Squamish out. This is an immigrant country. Over the next ten days the men stumble about the Squamish reserve on the north shore, building homes and suppressing a terrible urge to return to Snauq to see the charred remains. Swanamia watches as the men in her house fight for an acceptable response. Some private part of her knows they want to grieve, but there is no ceremony to grieve the loss of a village. She has no reference post for this new world where the interests of the immigrants precede the interests of Indigenous residents. She has no way to understand that the new people's right to declare us non-citizens, unless we disenfranchised our right to be Squamish, is inviolable. Khahtsahlano's head cocks to one side, he gives his wife a look that says "no problem, we will think of something" as the barge carries them out to sea. We are reserved and declared immigrants, children in the eyes of the law, wards of the government to be treated the same as the infirm or insane. Khahtsahlano is determined to fight this insult. It consumes his life.

We could not gain citizenship or manage our own affairs unless we forewent who we were: Squamish, T'sleil Waututh, Musqueam, Cree or whatever nation we came from. Some of us did disenfranchise. But most of us stayed stubbornly clinging to our original identity, fighting to participate in the new social order as Squamish.

The burning of Snauq touched off a history of disentitlement and prohibition that was incomprehensible and impossible for Swanamia to manage. We tried though. From Snauq to Whidbey Island and Vancouver Island, from Port Angeles to Seattle, the Squamish along with the Lummi of Washington State operated a ferry system until the Black Ball Ferry lines bought them out in 1930s.

Khahtsahlano struggled to find ways for us to participate. In 1905, he and a group of stalwart men marched all over the province of British Columbia to create the first modern organization of Aboriginal people. The Allied Tribes mastered colonial law despite prohibition and land rights to secure and protect their position in this country. He familiarized himself with the colonial relations that Britain had with other countries. He was a serious *rememberer* who paid attention to the oracy of his past, the changing present and the possibility of a future story. He stands there in this old photo just a little bent, handsomely dressed in the finest clothes Swanamia had made for him. His eyes exhibit an endless sadness. A deep hope lingers underneath the sadness softening the melancholy. In the photograph marking their departure, his son stands in front of him, back straight, shoulders squared with that little frown of sweet trepidation on his face. Khahtsahlano and his people faced the future with the same grim determination that the Squamish Nation Band council now deploys.

The wine grabs reality, slops it back and forth across the swaying room that blurs, and my wanders through Snauq are over for today.

A day later, slightly foggy from yesterday's wine, the hallways intervene again; I head for my office, cubby really. I am a teaching assistant bucking for my master's degree. This is a prestigious institution with a prestigious Master's program in Indigenous Governance. I am not a star student, nor a profound teaching assistant. Not much about me seems memorable. I pursue course after course. I comply day after day with research requirements, course requirements, marking requirements and the odd seminar requirements, but nothing that I do, say or write seems relevant. I feel absurdly obedient. The result of all this study seems oddly mundane. Did Khahtsahlano ever feel mundane as he trudged about speaking to one family head then another, talking up the Allied Tribes with

Andy Paull? Not likely, at the time he consciously opposed colonial authority. He too studied this new world but with a singular purpose in mind—recreating freedom in the context that I was to inherit. Maybe, while he spoke to his little sweetheart, enumerating each significant non-existent landmark, vegetable patch, berry field, elk warren, duck pond and fish habitat that had been destroyed by the newcomers, he felt this way. To what end, telling an eight-year-old of a past bounty that can never again be regained?

Opening the envelope begins to take on the sensation of treasonous behaviour. I set it aside and wonder about the course work I chose during my school years. I am Squamish, descendent from Squamish chieftains—no, that is only partly true. I am descendent from chieftains and I have plenty of Squamish relatives, but I married a Sto:loh, so really I am Sto:loh. Identity can be so confusing. For a long time, the T'sleil Waututh spoke mainly Squamish. Somehow they were considered part of the Squamish Band, despite the fact that they never did amalgamate. It turns out, they spoke downriver Halkomelem before the first smallpox killed them and later many began speaking Squamish. Some have gone back to speaking Halkomelem while others still speak Squamish. I am not sure who we really are collectively, and I wonder why I did not choose to study this territory, its history and the identity changes wrought on us all. My office closes in on me. The walls crawl toward me, slow and easy, crowd me. I want to run, to reach for another bottle of wine, but this here is the university and I must prepare for class—and there is no wine here, no false relief. I have only my wit, my will and my sober nightmare. I look up at the picture of Khahtsahlano and his son that adorns my office wall, the same picture that hangs in my living room at home. I must be obsessed with him. Why had I not noticed this obsession before?

I love this photo of him. I fell in love with the jackets of the two men, so much so that I learned to weave. I wanted to replicate that jacket. Khahtsahlano's jacket was among the first to be made from sheep's wool. His father's was made of dog and mountain goat hair.

Coast Salish women bred a beautiful long and curly haired dog for this purpose. Every summer the mountain goats left their hillside homes to shed their fur on the lowlands of what is now to be the "Sea to Sky Highway." They rubbed their bodies against long thorns and all the women had to do was collect the hair, spin the dog and goat hair together and weave the clothes. The settlers shot dogs and goats until our dogs were extinct and the goats were an endangered species. The object: force the natives to purchase Hudson's Bay sheep-wool blankets. The northerners switched to the black-and-red Hudson's Bay blankets, but we carried on with our weaving using sheep's wool for a time, then when cash was scarce, we shopped at local second-hand shops or we went without. Swanamia put a lot of love in those jackets. She took the time to trim them with fur, feathers, shells and fringe. She loved those two men. Some of the women took to knitting the Cowichan sweaters so popular among non-Indigenous people, but I could not choose knitting over weaving. I fell in love with the zigzag weft, the lightning strikes of those jackets and for a time, got lost in the process of weaving until my back gave out.

The injury inspired me to return to school to attend this university and to leave North Vancouver. I took this old archival photo—photocopy really—with me. Every now and then I speak to Khahtsahlano, promise him I will return.

My class tutorial is about current events; I must read the letter—keep abreast of new events and prepare to teach. I detach, open and read the notice of the agreement. I am informed that this information is a courtesy; being Sto:loh, I have no real claim to the agreement, but because ancestry is so important, all descendants of False Creek are hereby informed . . .

I look at the students and remember: This memory is for Chief George, Chief Khahtsahlano and my Ta'ah, who never stopped dreaming of Snauq. Song rolls out as the women pick berries near what is now John Hendry Park.

In between songs they tell old stories, many risqué and hilarious. Laughter punctuates the air, beside them are the biggest trees in the world, sixteen feet in diameter and averaging 400 feet in height. Other women at Snauq tend the drying racks and smoke-shacks in the village. Inside them, clams, sturgeons, oolichans, sockeye, and spring salmon are being cured for winter stock. Men from Squamish, Musqueam, and T'sleil Waututh join the men at Snauq to hunt and trap ducks, geese, grouse, deer and elk. Elk is the prettiest of all red meats. You have to see it roasted and thinly sliced to appreciate its beauty; and the taste, the taste is extraordinary. The camas fields bloom bounteous at Snauq and every spring the women cull the white ones in favour of the blue and hoe them. Children clutch at their long woven skirts. There is no difference between a white camas and a blue except the blue flowers are so much more gorgeous. It is the kind of blue that adorns the sky when it teases just before a good rain. Khahtsahlano's father, Khatsahlanogh, remembered those trees. On days when he carved out a new spoon, box or bowl, he would stare sadly at the empty forest and resent the new houses in its place. Chief George, sweet and gentle Chief George—Chipkayim—chose Snauq for its proximity to the mills and because he was no stranger to the place.

By 1907, the end of Chief George's life, the trees had fallen, the villagers at Lumberman's Arch were dead and the settlers had transformed the Snauq supermarket into a garbage dump. The newcomers were so strange. On the one hand, they erected sawmills in a disciplined and orderly fashion, transformed trees into boards for the world market quickly, efficiently and impressively. On the other hand, they threw things away in massive quantities. The Squamish came to watch. Many like Paddy George bought teams of horses and culled timber from the back woods like the white man. Well, not exactly like them: Paddy could not bring himself to kill the young ones—"space logging," they call it now. But still, some managed to eke out a living. Despite all the prohibition laws, they found some freedom in the context they inherited.

"The settlers were a dry riverbed possessing a thirst that was never slaked." A film of tears fills Khahtsahlano's eyes and his voice softens as he speaks. "After the trees came down, houses went up, more mills, hotels, shantytowns too, until we were vastly outnumbered and pressured to leave. B.C. was so white then. So many places were banned to Indians, Dogs, Blacks, Jews and Chinamans." At one time Khahtsahlano could remember the names of the men that came, first 100, then 1,000; after that, he stopped wanting to know who they were. "They were a strange lot, most of the men never brought *womans* to this place. The Yaletown men were CPR men, drifters and squatters on the north shore of the creek. They helped drain one third of it, so that the railroad—the CPR could build a station, but they didn't bring *womans*," he says as he stares longingly across the Inlet at his beloved Snauq.

I head to my class and enter. The students lean on their desks, barely awake. Almost half of them are First Nations. I call myself to attention: I have totally lost my professional distance from my subject; my discipline, my pretension at objectivity writhes on the floor in front of me, and I realize we are not the same people anymore. I am not in a Longhouse. I am not a speaker. I am a teaching assistant in a Western institution. Suddenly, the fluorescent lights offend, the dry perfect room temperature insults, and the very space mocks. A wave of pain passes through me; I nearly lunge forward fighting it.

Get a grip. This is what you wanted. Get a grip. This is what you slogged through tons of insulting documents for: Super Intendment of Indian Affairs, Melville, alternatives to solve the Indian problem, assassination, enslavement, disease, integration, boarding school, removal.

I am staggering under my own weight. My eyes bulge, my muscles pulse, my saliva trickles out the side of my mouth. I am not like Khahtsahlano. I am not like Ta'ah. I was brought up in the same tradition of change, of love of transformation, of appreciation for what is new, but I was not there when Snauq was a garden. Now it is a series of bridge ramparts, an emptied False Creek, emptied of Squamish people and occupied by industry, apartment dwellings, the Granville Island Tourist Centre and the Space Science Centre. I was not there when Squamish men formed unions like white men, built mills like white men, worked like white men and finally, unlike white men, were outlawed from full participation. I can't bear all this reality. I am soft like George but without whatever sweet thread of hope that wove its way through his body to form some steely fabric.

I awake surrounded by my students, their tears drip onto my cheeks. Oh my gawd, they love me.

"It's okay, I just fainted."

"You were saying you were not like Khahtsahlano, like Ta'ah. Who are they?"

The room opens up; the walls stop threatening. I know how Moses must have felt when he watched the sea part, the relief palpable, measurable, sweet and welcome.

"That's just it. I thought I knew who I was. I know the dates. I know the events, but I don't know who they were, and I can't know who I am without knowing who they were and I can't say goodbye to Snauq, but I need to say good bye. Oh gawd help me."

"Well, I am not real sure that clears things up," Terese responds, her blond hair hanging close to my face. Some of the students look like they want to laugh, a couple of First Nations students go ahead and chuckle.

"Snauq is a village we just forfeited any claim to, and I must say goodbye."

"Doesn't that require some sort of ceremony?" Hilda asks. She is Nu'chalnuth and although they are a different nation from mine, the ceremonial requirements are close.

"Yes," I answer.

"This is a cultural class, shouldn't we go with you?"

They lift me so tenderly, I feel like a saint. This is the beginning of something. I need to know what is ending so that I can appreciate and identify with the beginning. Their apathetic stares have been replaced by a deep concern. Their apathy must have been a mask, a mask of professionalism, a mask covering fear, a mask to hide whatever dangers lurk in learning about the horrors of colonialism. The students must face themselves. I am their teacher. The goal of every adult among us is to face ourselves, our greatest enemy; I am responsible as their teacher to help them do that, but I am ill-equipped. Still, Hilda is right. This is a cultural class and they ought to be there when I say goodbye. In some incomprehensible way, it feels as though their presence would somehow ease the forfeiture and make it right.

I conjure the stretch of trees to the west and south of Snauq for the class; the wind whispers songs of future to the residents. The Oblates arrive singing Gregorian chants of false promise. The millwrights arrive, singing chants of profit and we bite—hook, line and sinker. How could we anticipate that we would be excluded if our success exceeded the success of the white man? How could we know that they came homeless, poor, unsafe and unprotected? Yaletowners accepted their designation as "squatters." This struck the Squamish at first as incredible. Chief George had no way of perceiving of "squatting." It took some time for the younger men like Khahtsahlano to explain to Chief George the perception of "ownership" of the white man: the laws governing ownership, the business of property. Sometimes he resorted to English because the language did not suffice.

"B.C. is Indian land," but I have been speaking aloud.

"There is so much more to history than meets the eye. We need to know what happened and what happened has nothing to do with the dates, the events and the gentlemen involved, it has to do with impact." A sole student, eyes lifted slightly skyward, lips pursed innocent and inviting, strokes my arm.

They all pull their seats forward. "We need to finish this story."

They nod, like for the first time they seem to know what's going on. Even the white students nod, affirming that they too understand.

As I ready to head for the ferry terminal, it dawns on me that no one in this country has to deal with ancestry in quite the way we must. The new immigrants of today come from independent countries, some wealthy, some poor, but all but a few have risen from under the yoke of colonialism. They have nations as origins. Their home countries belong to the United Nations or NATO or other such international organizations. We do not and this court case indicates we never will. The United Nations is debating an Indigenous Right to Self-Government bill, but Indigenous people will never be able to acquire the place other nations hold. Canadians do not have to face that they are still classically colonized, that because settlement is *fait accompli*, we can only negotiate the best real-estate deal possible. Indigenous people must face this while the eyes of our ancestors, who fought against colonial conquest and lost, glare down upon us. "This is an immigrant nation," Prime Minister Chrétien said after the twin towers of the Trade Center in New York were felled. "We will continue to be an immigrant nation." How do we deal with this, the non-immigrants who for more than a century were rendered foreigners, prohibited from participation?

The money for Snauq will be put in trust. We must submit a plan of how we intend to spend it, to access it. The Squamish Nation gets to pick the trustees, but like our ancestors we must have trustees independent of our nation. Our money is still one step removed from our control.

This story is somehow connected to another story, more important than the one going on now. Surrender or dig up the hatchet. The Squamish Nation has chosen surrender. Which way will my journey take me? Do I dare remember Snauq as a Squamish, Musqueam, T'sleil Waututh supermarket? Do I dare desire the restoration of the grand trees to the left and in the rear of Snauq? Do I dare say goodbye?

The ferry lunges from the berth. Students surround. We are on a mission. We travel to Snauq, False Creek and Vancouver to say goodbye. In one sense I have no choice. In another, I chose the people who made the deal. In our own cultural sensibility there is no choice. There are 15,000 non-Indigenous people living at Snauq and we have never entitled ourselves the right to remove people from their homes. We must say goodbye.

In this goodbye, we will remember Snauq as it was before the draining of False Creek. We will honour the dead: the stanchions of fir, spruce, cedar and the gardens of Snauq. We will dream of the new False Creek, the dry lands, the new parks and the acres of grass and houses. We will accept what Granville Island has become and honour Patty Rivard, the First Nations woman who was the first to forge a successful business in the heart of it. We will struggle to appreciate the little ferries that cross the creek. We will salute Chief George—Chipkayim, Khatsahlanogh who embraced the vision of this burgeoning new nation. I will pray for my personal inability to fully commit to that vision.

The wind catches and lifts the tobacco as it wafts down to the water. As we watch it float, a lone Chinese woman crosses in front and smiles. I smile too. Li Ka Shing, a multi-billionaire, rose as the owner and developer of False Creek. He is Chinese and he didn't live here when he bought it. I don't know if he lives here now, but for whatever reason, I love the sound of his name. "Everything begins with song," Ta'ah says. His name is a song. It rolls off the tongue, sweetens the palate before the sound hits the air. It is such an irony that the first "non-citizen immigrant residents" should now possess the power to determine the destiny of our beloved Snauq. I know it shouldn't but somehow it makes me happy, like knowing that Black Indians now populate the Long Island Reservation in New York.

The Chinese were subjected to a head-tax for decades. Until sixty years ago they were banned from living outside Chinatown, though I met Garrick Chu's mother who grew up at Musqueam Reserve. They were restricted to laundry businesses and teahouses economically, once white men burned Chinatown to the ground.

For decades, Chinese men could not bring their families from China to Canada. Periodic riots in the previous century killed some of them and terrorized all of them. Underneath some parts of Chinatown, they built underground tunnels to hide from marauding white citizens who were never punished for killing Chinese. They endured quietly, like the Squamish, until assuming citizenship in 1948. For one of them to become the owner of this choice piece of real estate is a sweet irony. "It was sold for a song by Premier Vander Zalm," the court records read. That too is a piece of painful, yet poetic, justice. I want to attend the Chinese parade, celebrate Chinese New Year, not for Li Ka Shing, but because one of life's ironies has given me hope. On the other coast, 5,000 miles from here, a group of Mi'kmaq bought land in Newfoundland and gained reservation rights. Another irony. They thought they had killed them all, and 350 years later, there they were, purchasing the land and setting up a reservation. There is hope in irony.

I am not through with Canada. I am not a partner in its construction, but neither am I its enemy. Canada has opened the door. Indigenous people are no longer "immigrants" to be disenfranchised, forbidden, prohibited, outlawed or precluded from the protective laws of this country. But we are a long way from being participants. I am not anxious to be a part of an environmentally offensive society that can preach "thou shalt not kill" and then make war on people, plants and animals to protect and advance financial gain. The hypocrisy marring Canada's behaviour toward us is still evident, but she struggles for maturity and while she struggles, I accord myself a place. This place is still at the bottom, as the last people to be afforded a place at the banquet table, the attendees of which have been partaking for over 500 years, but still there it is, the chair, empty and hoping I will feel inclined to sit in it. The invitation is fraught with difficulties. Although today I must say goodbye, tomorrow I may just buy one of the townhouses slated for completion in 2010. Today, I am entitled to dream. Khahtsahlano dreamed of being buried at Snauq, I dream of living there.

We proceed to the unfinished Longhouse at the centre of Granville Island, a ragged group of students and their teacher. I break into song: Chief Dan George's Prayer Song. "Goodbye Snauq," I boom out in as big a voice as I can muster. The passing crowd jerks to a split-second halt, gives us a bewildered glance, frowns, sidesteps us and then moves on. The students laugh.

"Indians really will laugh at anything," I say as the tears stream across my face. The sun shines bright and turns the sky camas blue as we drift toward the Co-op restaurant to eat.

Raven has never left this place. Sometimes it feels like she has been negligent, perhaps she fell asleep and maybe never woke up. But Raven has not left this place.

Blessing Song

As the boat chugs away from the dock, the salt sea air surrounds us; it invades the very pores of our skin. The sun dances across the ocean's breast. Puget Sound, home of the giant octopus, resting place for the killer whale on its migration to California, is the garden of generations of Salish people. We are witnesses who have journeyed from the sky world to this place of continuous transformation, this place of physical engagement of the sea. Mountains rise sharp, snow-capped and deep green. They circle the sound, cradling this bowl of ocean that is very nearly landlocked. The depths of the sound comfort the whales; an abundance of sockeye and spring salmon attracts them here. Two of the longest and most powerful rivers on this continent drain into the sound.

We have come to watch the whales, my granddaughter, my daughter and myself. My daughter stands more erect than I have seen her stand for a long time, a smile etched on her face as she looks out toward the sea. She rocks gently back and forth, while her daughter darts about, taking pictures with her small camera—a gift from her aunt. Tania turns to look at me; the richness of her joy is contagious. We laugh out loud. We are where we were always meant to be, on a small boat plying the ocean waters off the west coast of British Columbia and Washington State.

It strikes me as odd that we have opted to take a holiday that is so modern and tourist-like, and yet we feel so old and so Salish for having done it. She slips her thin arm in mine, looks across at me, eyes brimming with tears of joy. We stay like that, rocking back and forth as though readying ourselves for song. The sun keeps climbing the skyline, nipping at our skin. The cool winds calm the heat of the sun as she reaches her noon zenith. My skin is browning under her glare, but it is not an unbearable heat. The other tourists scamper under the protection of the ship's canopy. They are white and so burn red under the brightness of the sun. Under the canopy, they engage one another in conversation about the beauty of the mountains, their awesome strength, but my girls and I quietly watch and wait.

The water slaps at the boat, the waves deepen as we come closer to the congregation. The boat rocks with a growing will. We look at one another and chuckle, our grip on one another's arm tightens. On the horizon, we see them, a super pod of resident killer whales. The water amplifies their resonant voices. There must be a hundred or more. The rocking of the boat intensifies; the waves caused by the gamboling and diving whales lick at the sides and threaten to douse the boat. The captain tells us the water is going to get rougher if we try to get closer, there are so many of them.

"What's your pleasure?" he asks.

"How much closer can we get without capsizing?" someone asks him.

"Let's see." He maneuvers the boat in the direction of the gathering.

"You may want to come inside," he hollers at us.

"Not a chance," we answer back at the same time and laugh.

My granddaughter stands behind us as though we could actually protect her. A small pod breaks away from the larger gathering and meanders toward the boat. The captain slows the boat down. The noisy tourists are now quiet. They lean toward the door of the cabin, clutching one another in silence. We stand pressed up against one another. The biggest of the whales swims within six feet of the boat, stands straight up and murmurs at us. The captain is stunned. "This has never happened before. He has never come this close to the boat." The songs of my people must have come from this whale.

I feel a song being pulled from some place deep inside me. I hesitate. We don't sing in front of white people, but the killer whale seems to demand nothing less.

The song emerges from my daughter and me as we stand there before this mammoth, both of us sing the oldest Salish song we know. The very moment the song ends, the whale slaps the water. The spray douses us and we break into that relieving sort of laughter that sloughs off all the agony of urban tension. He turns to join the super pod. His ladies follow him. We remain quiet and just stand there, arms still locked together. My granddaughter tells us that she has a picture of the big whale when he came up close to the boat. Her eyes sparkle with excitement. The people on board the boat are excited about what happened and curious about the song.

"It's just a song," we tell them. Neither of us is prepared to break the spell that this moment has created for us. This whale managed to close all the spaces between us. The song forced from us by the whale reminds us that our lineage stretches back forever. It isn't the song that matters though. What matters is the closing of the gap between us; the creation of oneness between three generations of Coast Salish women doing what every generation before us has done, standing in the middle of the sea singing to the whales.

Erotica

Before the explosion there is a quiet moment, a presence, delicate and warm, rich and heavy, a magic moment where sun touches skyline and paints the horizon fire-red, tangerine and yellow, when that skyline imprints its memory on your spirit forever. Before the explosion there is a feeling. It curls lazily along the contours of my back. It plays with my skin, touches me slowly. I can almost hear the feeling like a muted hush, a whisper calling my insides to pay attention. I am talking to someone else. I can see myself wrap up the conversation to create a deadened end. I feel myself turn, look past the face in the room. He is standing there, legs apart, very male; his body angled slightly, one hand adjusting his blue jeans, the other stroking his hair like he is getting ready for me. He's an elegant man, graceful, light-footed. I can feel my face change. Can feel my eyes drop their guard. A small smile forms—my lips part slowly. I start to censor myself, then decline. I said I wasn't going to do this to myself anymore. I shoot my censors. His eyes wander subtly over my body. The air jerks in my belly. Breathe deep. Don't shake. The room begins to disappear. The voices float into obscurity, disappear in a low murmur of irrelevance, taking so long to cross this room. He's studying me. Let him. I drop my last guard and open up. It's quite a can of miserable snakes running around in there, sir. Sure you really want to see? Inside, deep inside me, I want just one thing for even one moment: freedom, sensuous freedom, to love, to adore, to touch, to soak up the power and strength of manhood. He has no idea how deep this need to love is. Sure you want it, sir?

Sure you want someone who doesn't understand the meaning of failure, who has no ability to give up, who has dreamt of this moment for decades? Look at him. I see this small boy take charge of his world, bring his own laughter to it, watch him charm his way through painful moments alone. Watch him entrench stubbornly in moments of crisis. See this huge pushback against encroachment, this guillotine that can sever him from even those who love him. Do I want this? Old Man hovers in the background, smiling. He whispers it's okay. In the end, I never let him down. I own the wisdom of his ages. In the face of real affection I soothe his hardness, pull up on the reins of his stubbornness. Just be real. His eyes soften, wrap themselves around me, excite. Not here. Not here. Pull out the stops. I reach for his hand and say my name. There is a caress in my voice, the caress I put into my voice when I read poetry. It has never slipped out on its own like that. "Is this your cute and coy routine?" he asks all sweet and seriously smiling. I blush inside, deep in my belly. I let it play in my abdomen for a while. I have no routines, just emotions. He takes my shoulder in his hands. It burns where he touches. His heart is in this hot touch. A warm summer tide slides into the shore of my own watery beachhead. A wash of gentle wind rushes over me and the tidal wave of desire I had carefully kept in a thin glass bottle of hope shatters. Inside my belly it explodes. My womanhood, damned up for decades, bursts. His voice rich with bedroom promise tells me it's alright to be standing in the middle of a crowded room, all wet, pulsing and wanting from that place. The shame, the years of shame that kept my desire bottled up, dissipates, leaks out with the hot fluid messing my underwear. I can see myself in his eyes. I look so soft, so pliable, so full of surrender. I have to let go of his hips. He slides his hand out from my shoulder. He takes his time. The lingering hand barely touches my breast as it releases me. We're still staring at one another. Our movements now have acquired a common rhythm, a grace all our own. This man could take me on some roller coaster ride. He could also hurt me—really hurt me. I tell my voice of caution to hush up. I have been hurt. My life has been filled with it. I have no memories to alleviate the hurt, to ameliorate the depth of it, to soften the memory of it. This man can give me joyful memories to crowd out the pain. I want those memories. I need them. I need to feel this love swell my womanhood. I want it to fill my belly, send my body crazy. I want to experience this desire full-blown and wild. I want to surrender to his touch, his voice, his desire. I want to satiate my womanly affection under the dome of his manhood. Please me . . . please . . . please.

Friend introduces us. He tells her we have already met. My friend's voice should have cracked the reverie. It doesn't. I am already in too deep. "Where shall we go?" I could care less. Just now, I would go anywhere with him. Let someone else more conscious than I decide. He names a place. I mumble something that resembles an affirmation, tell myself I am crazy, agree with my diagnosis, but I follow him. I am going to go right over the edge. I'm going to love the free fall.

A dim memory returns: of jumping off the old shed roof. The shock of nothing there to break my fall returns, sharp, insistent. No grass. My knees lock on impact. I lie there still in pain, pray for someone to come. My voice moves to scream—pain seizes it, stops it. The movement is too much. I lie stock-still and wait. Someone will come. No one comes. The sun begins to drop. Darkness crowds the light.

The sun setting against the salt chuck below mocks my lonely wait. Never again. No more free-falls. The light dances atop the tiny waves, winking sadistically. Tears leak from my eyes. I'm careful not to sob; the muscle action will restore the pain. It's mainly dark now. The old maple below is casting shadows over the grass. A thin line of red against the skyline is all that's left. Wind tosses the giant leaves of the maple back and forth. The greying shadows deepen and finally disappear. A familiar voice and a dependable touch rescues me. It's my brother; he unlocks my knees murmuring words of encouragement to me. One scream and the pain is gone. I only had to straighten out my legs. How embarrassing.

"When you fall down girl, get up," I tell myself. Will I be able to get up? I will never know until after the fall. Is he worth the glory of the free-fall if the landing is hard and cold like the hours spent waiting? The free-fall is worth it. Watch him hold our mutual friend. She can see. I know this about her. She adores him. He must be worth adoring. That isn't the point. No one has to love you. So far no one has, not any man anyway. Some have adored me, most have idolized me, worn me like a merit badge. Some have wanted me, imaged up erotica and spurred their lust into tender words, used me as a vessel for their own satisfaction. Some have sought the calm they believe is omnipresent, as though having a woman would quiet the internal war going on inside and bring them eternal peace. None have loved the crazy fire that burns bright inside me.

The fire that hothouses my desire is the same fire that pushes up this peace, this knowing that "this too shall pass." I know what the water looks like when men try to quiet your insatiable thirst for knowing. The desire and the knowing come from the same fire. Push on his need to quiet your fire. Hold bones in my hand. Old Lahal bones—a king and queen—a mating pair. I caress the bones and ready myself for a good game of Lahal. A good bone game player knows there is no gambling in Lahal. It's about seeing, about reading the faces on the other side of the fire, about patience, about belief in the process and not measuring the product—not loving the win but the journey through the game. The game is about looking at everything there. It's about dropping all your guards, travelling to the whirlwind of see, and opening up to the storm of vision without refuge. Don't cheat. Your complexity, your simplicity, your hope and despair, your anger and affection, your courage and fear—all will be seen.

Don't hide. Throw out my marriage vows, set them carefully on the table of the café. He sets them aside. They have no meaning to him. He knows they are a lie. I have a marriage but it's obvious I have no love. It's clear to him. I'm telling him this, so he knows what he's dealing with. We play. I gush; he pushes harder. He's relentless, determined to fire me up. He wants to see how far he can take me, how much desire lives inside this woman. How much he can pull up. There's a song in his throat, sultry and seductive. I hear the rhythm, the melody overtop his laughter. It echoes through my body. Picture myself touching his skin, breathing overtop his body, my lips skirt the surface of him, travel to his manhood and enjoy, enjoy—his body.

My friend watches. A look of deep concern is on her face. She wonders what the hell has come over me. She has never seen me this alive, this completely free. It must look crazy from her side of the table. She knows I am married. The question of my marriage lingers on her face reminding me of my revulsion for it. It's been over a year. He lives in one town; I live in another. I found a moment to mention that. Did he say something about my husband? What was the line that pushed up this little fact? Was I just making a confession? I remember saying I had a perfect marriage; he lives a couple of hundred miles away. I don't remember what came before. Touch his arm, his leg, tease him, tell him about my life. I can feel his body right through his clothes. My friend looks at him, at me, back at him, back at me. She is still worried.

There is going to be some hell to pay. The hell of him deciding not to have me, or the hell of him deciding to go ahead. Either way, there is going to be some hell to pay. The laughter, my husband's face appears. His frailty becomes so obvious. His need to linger in the shadows of my public life freezes me. His rage at my betrayal will be big. He will wail on me. I may not survive. I may not be able to fight back.

I want this moment, just this moment. I lean my leg against his; a flame of hot desire licks the inside of my leg where it touches his. "You owe your husband your life," I say to myself like some lawyer arguing on his behalf. He rescued you from death, worked overtime while you struggled to live. Gratitude makes an ugly bedmate. You know you can't stand having him help himself to you, relieve himself with your body. He can not see you are not enjoying his love at all. I make a lousy whore. I tried. I'm not going back. I'll have dreams instead. I know what they look like. Intensity drops, his voice changes, softens, becomes not a hot prod pushing up desire but a gentle wind soothing, bringing me from satisfaction to peace. I can't go back.

This decision did something for me. It was as though he had made love to me and now it was time to bathe in the glow of it, let the warmth nestle about us, brings us closer to one another. In the dark quiet of my friend's room, turning over what had happened to me, Shirley Valentine came back. I fell in love with me. It was not so much him. It was about loving my present. Ambitions and survival are not enough. I want full banquet living, full textured life, with all its bumps, obstacles and fire. Maybe, I still want him too.

The Café

A bell announces every customer; its bragging little ding celebrates the fact that some fool deliberately decided to dine out in this lousy excuse for a diner. The man at the cash looks up, inspects the old woman who shuffles through the door as though he has the right to assess the worthiness of a prospective customer. He has a lot of nerve perching on his imagined pedestal, playing judge in this place. He ought to be glad that anyone bothers to come in. This is Carrall and Hastings. The café is right across from the Sunrise, a hotel of considerable disrepute. The café is located in the heart of skid row. Outside, people stagger to and fro, not from home to work but back and forth between Main and Carrall because they have no home. They beg spare change from passersby so they can come in here for a bowl of soup, a cup of coffee, a minute or two of relief from the rain, the street, the other beggars, the nothingness of their lives, anything at all. This part of the row might just as well be a million miles from a money-making business. No money can be made here because the people in this neighbourhood have none. This is the place that neighbours forming hoods protect their children from. This is the place we warn our children about. Just two blocks west, there is another diner much more spacious; the seats are plump and comfortable, the food ordinary but not greasy. Here, the cook is not. He is just a guy collecting minimum wage, passing time, waiting until he hits some magical year in which he is too old to get up in the morning, even to throw hamburgers or fries on a grill or stir soup.

Heavy porcelain mugs, squatting stoutly over thick saucers, separate us from one another. Their stoutness stills the wildness that threatens the air between us. It frays the sensuousness of the still moments, ices up those silky movements of his, and freezes my desire—mid-air. Vapour twists itself above the cup. I can't believe the coffee in this place is hot; ah, must be the coldness of the restaurant that makes the coffee look so warm and inviting.

The bare bulb above and to the north of us glares, its hundred-watt globe bears down on us as though to interrogate our motives, question the very morality of our presence in this café. Its bright nakedness accuses.

He looks—intent. He is going to bring up personal feelings regarding another teacher or a student. One he doesn't like. He thinks I might care because I appear to like him. For some people, saying you don't like someone automatically provokes the listener to become an ally siding with the speaker in whatever imaginary warfield they are playing on. I lift an eyebrow. I am suspicious, but not very game for internecine war.

An old tape goes off in my head. It's from an anthropology class some fifteen years earlier: "Indians have fat on their eyelids." I want to reach up and touch my eyelid to test the validity of the instructor's remark. I did not know that. "It marks . . ." I stifle my laugh. Murphy Green hisses in my ear from behind me, "I didn't come here to learn about ear wax—honey-coloured or otherwise—or fat on my f'king eyes." As twenty sets of near-blue eyes subtly try to ascertain whether or not this bizarre statement is true, Murphy's words inspire a deeper desire to howl with laughter. "It's twoo, it's twoo," he mocks. "I have fat eyelids," looking directly at the young man who was staring at us. The student's face reddened and he turned his shame toward the instructor.

Now I stare hard at my date, fighting down the laugh. He scowls, like he knows I am about to crack up. The scowl sits awkward across the burnished velvet of his skin stretched taut over cheekbones so high they obscure the loveliness of his eyes, but only momentarily.

He stirs his coffee, dragging the spoon with care from one end of the cup to the other. Just to the left of this dangerous game he is about to play, there is a sense of self that warns him that the game is not dignified. His dignity, however, is quiet. Still, it interferes with his attempt to abdicate his scowl in favour of the game. While this quarrel takes shape on his face, his mask falls off and his eyes articulate desire. He catches himself—the soft scowl returns. It hovers about his brow, but fails to curl his lips. His lips are full and square, mauve hued brown, and elicit desire in me despite the game.

"She's your friend, this student." The air shifts. He drops the sentence, leaves it unfinished on purpose; its very leanness wants me to fill in the blank notes of his discontent with small bits of disaffection toward her that I may have buried inside. It is a warning. It hints of a current, an undertow, that will drown both of us. It invites me to conjure the space between his missing lines, fill them with my own doubt, turn them into lacerations that will shred my friendship and render suspect my friendly feelings for her. I know of whom he speaks. She has no ill feeling toward him, is friendly in fact, believes them to be on good terms. But I have seen how difficult it is for him to be civil to her, as though she brings out the worst in him. Some piece of him has decided she does this in a planned way.

The light above no longer accuses. His words are crass, but his eyes have softened like the light. They are not part of his current conversation. I am barely able to pay attention to his words overtop the delivery of promise in his eyes and the silk soft smoothness of his movements. I can't tell him this. He's aware he's good looking. His good looks have gotten him in and out of trouble. He looks embattled, but he has fought this battle before and won. He lets his voice go, released by lips pursed sensual, lustful. The sound of it is a murmur, throaty and full, a meticulous blend of English brushed gently across an ancient accent. It shapes his words into a strangely seductive symphony, raspy and tempered with confidence. The beats, the chords all persuade that his disdain is harmless. It lacks treachery, but I know better and I have no interest in this game of gangsterism and allegiance over distaste and dislike.

"She really pushes my buttons." A swell of urgency heightened by his disblief in her ability to overtake his calm, his near shock at the craft of overwhelming she has mastered, and its effect on him, pierces the melody of his voice. I resent the sound he now makes. He is too old to pretend not to know that he shouldn't have any buttons left to push at his age. He really should be over himself. I knock back my coffee.

"Would you like more?" The music returns, his voice a purr.

Yes I want more, much more.

"More coffee?" The waitress's strident voice cracks the cadence of his symphony between his breaths of sound—good thing. He jerks, slightly surprised she interrupted him. He focuses his eyes on his cup, pushes it forward after a second.

"Sure," he breathes, then looks at me. I believe he knows that he elicits desire from me. I picture him doing so with careful deliberation. He turns his head slightly, cocks it to one side as his eyes follow mine. Some men are so pretty they hurt to look at. His profile neat and perfect—aristocratic lines—the pose impresses me. I manage to push my cup forward, then involuntarily lean into his conversation without taking my eyes off his face. The waitress fills my cup. The muscles in my face tighten. Heat is flirting with my womb. I want to curse. The heat sooths my gaze. My voice softens, takes on a bedroom quality. It brings some kind of curled confidence up in me. I am going to shift his attention, use the shift to alter his course. I don't even consider losing his friendship, his desire, into the equation.

"Write it. I want to see it in a poem."

Peace curls about my toes
slides up my leg
stops inside my belly   dances
A single wave of lust swallows the peace, crests, gushes, recedes.
I uncross and re cross my legs and stare at my cup.

"I know it's inside me. The place she pushes up is mine but I can't help can't like her." The rhythm of his pauses is foreign. I want to ask him if he ever had trouble with commas.

"Just put a comma whenever you pause," I hear my tutor. It took years for me to figure it out.

We don't pause in the same places as the others. I gave up on commas periods too. Just leave a space. I'm smiling. His eyes play with my smile. I conjure a response. I can see him getting ready for a fuller piece of conversation.

I listen underneath his words, commit them to memory and move beyond the moment to the tide. Naughty sea on sand lolls forward. I watch it caress sand, rearrange its ridges, move the sand, one grain at a time, rock it back and forth, forth and back, then deposit it in some valley below the ridge. I feel the curved line of water fold in on itself.

"*Khyeh*," he breathes a chuckle, licks his lips, his tongue barely perceptible. The smile stretched only at the edges of his mouth.

My tongue is dry. I sip.

The line rolls up from under a bowl of sea green, pales as it rises to meet sky. Under sun's glare, the fringes of white tips crest atop the paled green tunnel—a cylindrical sheet of deep green moves toward the white froth. A cool sheet falling against hot burnt skin.

"Coffee? Hot?" he asks. The "Hot?" all by itself alone becoming its own question.

"Yes," I breathe. Hot. Yes hot. Coffeehot. I clear my throat. "Yes."

A small moment of shock hot pleasant then cool
body moves from intense
heat to peaceful warm
His words roll above the seasounds, play above the tide's
tendrils wend their way over the tempest in my womb
soothes the shock.

I listen from within the maelstrom of the sea's storm   stare at his face—at the veil of dream image. We both lean catch ourselves straighten up. I float above the friction that is sand, paint dream images over the structural reality of his face, sway so slightly lightly forth back hot cool back forth. My insides swell soften threaten to tighten.

Leathery seats. The seats are leather. Feel the leather. Become aware of leather. Clutch the real moment the dry as dust moment the dispassionate moment. The game moment. The cup in front of me wants attention.

Pay attention.

"More coffee?" The waitress sobers me up.

Breathe. Breathe regular breath deep breathe   normal. I stare at dark chocolate colour. The vapour lets go of my cup whirls above it.

"Yes." Come on Lee. You have more words in your vocabulary than "yes—yes—yes" and for a moment it seems possible. If I could just find a way to frame an affair in colours which are not sordid,

dull colours
murky colours
colours full of ambivalence thin out become veneers to cover
lawless voids
dreamless colours
furtive colours skulk unseen between the light of the cafe
and the dark inside me melts.

Moments of joy sandwiched between hiding the heat under cool colours of table tops, plain seats and thick mugs of coffee. Joy squeezed tight between journeys through body truth—kinesis—my body remains honest insists on voluptuous truth my voice razored tempered by conscience and social dictum utters another truth under which I stand. This dome of understanding wags its finger at me

(I am sorry Lee—body—sentient Lee—I can't do this)

The cup of liquid holds his lips for a moment the whisps of steam open up as two twin vapour trails part and let go of the warm clay edge. His lips release his cup's edge. He looks up. His lips, still slightly parted and his cup perched in mid-air, carefully coddled by his hand.

Release the cup. Rhythmically it sways, fullsome to the command of finely chiselled fingers. The fog of steam reaches skyward. Plump at the open neck of the cup the vapour dances up, thins before it dissipates. I look away. I turn my eyes toward my own cup. Against the warm brown of my coffee lies the lingering image of his face and hands coffee coloured under a bronze hue with the slightest hints of red which play about the skin of them. The coffee frees itself. Sip by sip the steam escapes. Whisp by whisp the cup is drained, while I sit suspended between desire and old codes that live entrapped in my consciousness.

These codes fray at the edges torn slightly by desire, but the cloth of them holds fast. Too bad he is stuck with the need for forming mobs. Games of gang up.

> blood thickens, cools, clots,
> as it journeys away from my womb.

"Why don't you write it out of your system?" I say it aloud. He thinks my words are for him. It echoes, bounces off the walls of old codes that paralyze my wayward inner self. He stares, looks down at his cup, looks up from under eyebrows just a hint of black against red brown. His head bends down one last time. One eye partly closed, the other looking slightly up, an open invitation. The words rasp across his full mouth too sweet, too soft and way too slow.

"Yeah—maybe I should." My body riots. Don't look at him—write it—write it—we have laws—write it—Jeezusss—I close my eyes. My fingers clutch the cup too tight. The cup's squat shape shakes under my clutch. My fingers relax I swallow the contents. Its fat form—this cup—she's too stout for desire to swallow good sense.

I want to tell him it is a question of law—of power—not desire—he might talk me out of it—it wouldn't take much. Instead I throw my jacket on while he dons his pack, gives me a moment of hesitation to consider all the possibilities. I catch his image only peripherally. My eyes stare at the cup covering my mouth, that I drain as I stand up to leave. I can hear his sigh, so subtle, controlled and sadly buried.

Laundry Basket

The laundry basket is full again. The wicker basket is old, its sides bursting in spots. She mentally promises to buy a new one—when her financial situation has altered. It's number forty-two on the old list of priorities. She forgets how, but somehow the basket had been bent so that it leaned to the side instead of standing up straight. Soiled shirts and overalls form a mound on top. A stiff little sock sits perched on the edge of the clothes, barely hanging onto the rest of the laundry. Nothing seems to be holding it to the stack. She shuts the bathroom door on the laundry scene very carefully so as not to jar the sock loose. She ignores the little voice inside her calling her to tend the laundry.

It's mid-day. The sun overhead whispers, pale, shadowless light. The yard outside the window is bright, but inside it's a little dull. Only morning light shines into the old living room. The first draft is done and she pulls the last sheet from the typewriter, then pours herself a coffee. "Coffee. Poison really." But she has so precious few vices. "No excuse." It's kind of like the laundry in reverse. She knows she should do a load, but it's mid-day, too late to begin a major overhaul of the family wardrobe. She should just do it. Coffee is poison, she should just quit doing it, but she neither does what she ought to, nor stops doing what she ought not to. It seems misbehaviour is her reward for freeing herself of domination.

The voice nags on: The kids will need clean clothes for school—turn the damn things inside out. This isn't the reserve—there was a time when we weren't so gawdamned concerned about other people's opinions. This isn't 1950—she tells herself to shut up, and starts proofing her last piece. The walls pulse. The floor starts to sway; the food-print on the wallpaper squeezes his memory from behind its gaudy pictures.

"My mother held a job and did the laundry, too." The quality of his voice has changed. During his endless complaining about her unwillingness to work and work and work, his voice had been loud and arrogant. Now in its dreamy memory state it possesses a mocking purr as though, from wherever in the world he was, he knew she was not keeping up with the holy duties of motherhood.

"Get out." She threatens the silent walls as though he were really there. The very pattern of the paper seems to hold her past intact. He chose the paper, like the laundry basket—"Wicker is natural," he had said against her desire for plastic. "Yeah, natural and unclean-able." She now remembers how the damned thing got its wow in it. She had washed it in hot water and the wicker had warped. She is mad all over again. And the obnoxious wallpaper choice, she didn't know why he wanted a pattern of food, loud and raw, to adorn the kitchen. She hadn't said anything at the time, but now tears rested just behind her eyes, threatening to roll out onto the machine. She could have said, "No." No to the wallpaper, no to the wicker, but she knew she could not say no to having to do the laundry, mother the children and him, and somehow that seemed so pathetic. Pathetic because she had lived with it for so long and he had left without ever realizing how tyrannical that was.

She looks up at the old clock. "Two hours, I still have time," she soothes herself. "What am I doing? He's gone but his voice still dictates my every mood. It hangs thick in the air, loud like the paper." The words are whispered out loud. They try to squeeze themselves between the designs on the wall as she tries to shove the memory back into the grapes, vegetables and bread hanging off the plain white paper. "Whoever heard of bright gold grapes, yellow bread or sharp green tomatoes and carrots?" That remark erases his presence.

Her hand is still clutching the cup of, now, cool coffee. On the side of the cup is written "Decision Maker." The lip of the cup is well chipped. Hepatitis can be contracted from chipped stoneware, she had read somewhere, and reminds herself to add new dishes to her list of priorities. Number forty-three. She had gotten them for a birthday in the days when things were going well between them. Well for him that is. To be truthful, things had been magical for both of them in those first few years. She had done her household duties with enthusiasm, actually believing that her obligations as wife were her source of joy. Decision maker. The irony of the gift now strikes her.

In fact, he had left most of the household decision making up to her for those years. It was when she had stepped out of the bounds of orthodoxy that he had "put his foot down" or rather began putting the back of his hand across her face. She wanted to remember the precise moment, the pivotal point of her change.

The clock rolled backward across her memory and Choklit Park came into view. She was staring at them all: her husband, her children and a friend of theirs, all rough-housing, sliding and swinging on the toys at the park. From the hill, she could see False Creek and the memory of Khahtsahlano rolled into focus. He was staring across the water from a hillside in North Vancouver, pining to be buried in his lost homeland. She was a little girl, just like her eldest son, but instead of swinging on swings or hanging from bars, she was listening to an old man. The children and her husband receded. Silence, but for old Khatsahlano's voice. And finally the picture of the park changed. Vancouver was still so new then. Bush adorned the edges of the inlet right up to the sugar refinery.

Now it's roadway and park—Brighton Park and deep-sea vessels. The Vancouver Hotel bragged about being the tallest building; now you can't even see it from the other side. False Creek was just a marina and a barrel company during the last days of Khahtsahlano; now it is the most densely populated area in the city. Prime real estate. It was funny to hear them say that as though land could be likened to beef—prime real estate, prime rib roast. Khahtsahlano could not write. His face faded and the children returned.

She had made her decision then. Shortly after that, she had gone out and bought an unabridged dictionary and had begun the tedious process of looking up parts of speech—English grammar construction. She had been noting them in an exercise book for some time. On the trail to recovering language she had come across a host of words interesting in themselves; she had played with her thoughts in little scribbles.

The crunching sound of mail sliding through the old slot breaks the pattern of her thought. "More bills." Reluctantly, she reaches to the floor where the bent envelopes sit in disarray. There just isn't a way to toss letters through a skinny slot without crunching them up and having them land in a position of indignity. "Disarray, like the damn laundry, the wallpaper and my life."

The hum of the typewriter overtop the soft shuffling of the envelopes reminds her that she had chosen to purchase a writing machine instead of a washing machine. "Not very thrifty. Too late now." She is broke and considers pawning the typewriter. "What would it be like not to be able to kick out story after story for the rejection of editor after editor? I'll die if I don't keep pecking and believing . . ."

The last scene between Grant and her returns. Papers, piled one on top of the other, crinkled up in the tub and then the match set fire to them all. A scream had rolled up from the bottom of her feet, grew in intensity and threatened to swallow her. It had stopped at her heart. It was too big. The howl snapped her to attention.

"You want to burn this, do you? You want to burn—my life. You want to burn—the inside of me, and the soul of me. Burn me? Me?" And she had reached into the laundry basket and hauled shirt after shirt out and then thrown them onto the paper pyre in the tub. He yelled. Momentarily caught by surprise, he had hesitated long enough for the edges of the soiled shirts to char. He tried to rescue a shirt by pouring water on the fire, then backhanded her. It seemed like a single motion. It had been enough.

After that, it didn't take him long to disappear. She had been surprised at the swiftness of her next few decisions: the injunction, the charges, the inability of the police to find him, then the divorce—a whirlwind storm of decision making. She had not realized how devoted she was to her stories. "What had brought it all on?" Most of her pieces had been harmless little bits of entertainment for the kids. Some she gave away to friends. She remembered Sara. Sara had been the one to leave when her marriage broke up. Now she was moving back home to take care of her teenaged children whose father had given up trying to raise them, leaving them to her in disgusted frustration. The customs of divorce had all changed in the last while. Men were gaining custody of young children, then as the problems of biochemical teenage revolution fell on them, they were returning them to their mothers. She had several friends riding in this canoe and Sara was special among them.

She wanted to give her something, something intensely personal, something of her soul. A story that was close to her heart. Sara knew about publishers and had sent the story to some magazine. They wanted it. That's all it took. The possibility of turning her life and the lives of hundreds of other unknowns to account had inspired her. Inspired her in a way no man, woman or child could.

Scribbling became an obsession. When she wasn't scribbling she was reading. Story after story came off the typewriter in clean, neat rows. They circled through her insides and became part of her. His rage, his omnipresence shrank as her passion for her own words grew. He objected. She resisted. Sneaking about during the day, she wrote furtively, secretly. She saved time by not caring so much about housework. Wall-washing was sacrificed to writing. Deleting daily floor washing added to writing time. She took to washing dishes only during the half hour before he returned home from work. She accumulated time the way misers save money, moment by moment, penny by penny. She let the laundry pile up week after week until there were no clean clothes left in the house and she absolutely had to wash or get caught.

Get caught? How absurd her lifestyle then seemed. "Get caught." Like somehow her lack of devotion to housework was some crime. She felt guilty leaving the poor old socks in the basket until she had no choice but to haul them to the laundromat. "Poor old socks." Still, she scribbled and scribbled. She sent envelope after envelope out to magazines. She even bought a *Canadian Writer's Guide*. Very few of her imagination's journeys seemed to fit into the editorial plans of magazine publishers. Romance among Indigenous people is so subtle that Canadians would not recognize a love story about us if they fell on it. Still, she carried on.

Most times she never heard from the people again, but once in a while an editor's note would come back: Too narrow a genre; not marketable; take the drinking out; the violence is too raw for our audience; no one will purchase a magazine with stories about child sexual abuse. The answers spurred her on. No one said the writing was bad. It was her choice of subject they didn't care for. "Someday, our lives will interest you, Canada, and I will have a host of angels just waiting for you to read . . ."

The stories got closer, sharper, more vivid and more honest. Finally, he crept into them. His rage, the stupidity of feminine bondage and male dominance rolled out on the crisp, white sheets. She had couched the essence of him in fiction, but he was still recognizable. He went to work as usual, she suspected nothing. He returned home and found her as available and almost as devoted as usual. He was smug about his victory over her silly obsession. He even made fun of her dreams by perusing the entertainment section of the paper and reading reviews of new works.

"Wouldn't you like to be one of these guys, Marla? Look here, another new book. Of course, this one is written by a real writer." She cringed, remained silent and finally grew distant, almost immune to his remarks.

One Friday, he had returned an hour or so early and found the lot. She hadn't been there at first. She wondered now what his face had looked like when he read her story, saw himself and began crumpling sheet after sheet. She wondered if he had paced all about the house, through the kitchen looking for the right receptacle, deciding on the tub. The tub. It was the tub in which she had helped her children burn pictures of their nightmares. Maybe it was all too nightmarish for him, a white man, to see this Indian bride become one of the pampered literati of Canada. The sickening notion struck her that he had fallen in love with her because he wanted someone to whom he could feel superior.

She had come back from the next-door neighbour's in time to watch the lot burn. She saw herself going up in smoke. The word "*fire*" ignited her insides. His shirts, his precious shirts, the ones he so carefully selected, tailored to fit, as though they expressed his very soul. She had watched her hands commit the crime and in some strange way had felt lusty for the first time in a long time.

Even through his backhand she had wanted to laugh, a sultry, deep-throated, full and lusty laugh. It scared her now. It dawned on her, maybe he had figured it out. Maybe he had become so incensed because he associated her dwindling sensuousness with her increased writing. It felt creepy, sexually perverse, for him to sense something about her sensuality and its relationship to writing before she had come to realize it. She felt as though she had just been told that someone was watching her undress every night without her knowing it.

Her hands stop shuffling the mail. They rest themselves on a cheque. The cheque was waiting for her to pay attention. She tears the thing open, letting the other letters fall to the floor. "Edie's Courtship" had made it. The cheque and the prospect of a second-hand Hoover washer crowded the memories out. She waves the cheque in triumph. The laugh she couldn't utter under her ex-husband's backhand bursts forth.

The old station wagon she had bought with her last cheque stands out front, lonely from lack of use. She grabs her keys and climbs in, grinds the beast into gear and heads for Joe's Used Appliance yard at the end of the alley.

Joe likes seeing her come in. She never buys anything, but he likes seeing her anyway. She is glorious. Thin. Reedy, big-eyed and full of smiles. Unconsciously, he draws a breath and holds it in his gut before swaggering in her direction.

"She's on a roll, Joe. Money. A cheque. I'll take that Hoover washer over there, if you will trust me with this cheque." She was laughing, looking lovelier then ever. Joe joins her. He takes a look at the cheque.

"Mac and Steward, not bad. Are they going to publish the whole book?"

"The whole damn thing," she answers. "This is a lot of money. I better make sure I can cash it." She hugs him. He spins her around. The Hoover stood, saying "Buy me." She feels a little weepy. No more rude laundresses breaking up her reading to tell her, "Your MA-chine IS ready."

From the till, Joe mentions her needing the dryer. The one is not much good without the other. "Oh Gawd," she thinks and the grating stress of decision-making is upon her again, new wallpaper and a table and chairs or a damn dryer. Joe is right; the little washer isn't much good without the dryer, but if she takes the dryer the wallpaper that hid his image in the harmless gaudy print of food will have to stay. Hot rage boils inside. How could a man spend thirty bucks a crack on dozens of shirts while his family went without a table and chairs? And with his wife rolling off once a week harnessed to a shopping cart to a laundromat whose laundress could hardly tolerate her race, he'd drive to work in his new car.

The portrait of her kitchen, in the middle of which sat an old drum with a piece of plywood nailed to it, returns. She wants to cry.

She stares hard at Joe. Within the pale of his skin, his blue eyes, the mass of light brown hair playing on his face rests the answer. She has half a notion to ask him, but his joy tells her not to.

At the bottom of her ex-husband's obsession with tailored shirts and his own transport taking precedence over family needs is this. Her husband had never brought any of his workmates to their house. It dawned on her, he had never intended to let anyone he respected know what his wife looked like—hot shame crowded her mind. Joe knows. Joe's people know. She told herself that this was ridiculous. How could Joe be blamed for her ex-husband's quirks? She hated saying "ex-husband"—as though you could never divorce the memory of marriage.

The courtroom scene of her divorce returns. She re-listens to the judge, relives the solemnity of the moment. He was old, white. His voice filled the room, but it was cold. He held a silly hammer in his hand—a gavel, she now knew. She had wanted him to give her some instructions, to say something profound. Instead he simply granted her a divorce in unadorned flat language and then dismissed her with his gavel. Her husband had not contested the divorce or application for custody. No complications except the tight feeling inside her wanted to say, "Excuse me, I just divorced your entire race, your honor, wouldn't you like to comment on that? I mean, I chucked out his entire lineage as a possible source of comfort in the hereafter, so wouldn't you like to resent that for just a moment?"

"Are you okay?" She snaps out of her daze to Joe's face looking curiously at her. She wonders how long her thoughts had taken. Long enough for Joe to notice, anyway.

"I got to stop doing this. I was just daydreaming, conjuring up another story. Are you divorced, Joe?"

"Oh yeah. Who isn't these days?" He gets shy, less brassy, like he is hoping there is something for him in the question. She decides not to pursue it any further. She can't tell him that he is a nice guy

but she has already divorced his entire race. Best not get into a position where she would have to tell the truth if the truth was too ugly
for the listener to understand.

"Put the dryer in the wagon, Joe." She turns to leave. She doesn't
get far. Joe calls out after her, wondering how she thinks she is going
to get the dryer from the car to her apartment.

She thinks of her sons. "We'll manage," she answers, cautiously
curt. She smiles back gratefully and carries on. At the house she has
to wait until her boys return. Between the three of them, the assistance of an Egyptian jack and a whole lot of grunting effort, plan-
ning, re-planning and making judicious use of muscle and leverage
smarts, the three of them manage to get the two machines into the
apartment.

Joe had given her change for the cheque. She clung to the bills,
a ten and a twenty. Now she decides to order pizza. "Go to hell
walls," she murmurs as she dials 222-2222. While waiting for the
pizza man, the two boys load the little Hoover and turn it on. Another milestone. She hadn't thought of that. It never occurred to
her that for the boys, laundry is not looked upon as "woman's work,
wifely drudgery, not fit for male consumption." It is new and they
want to be a part of it.

"Ooh, yuck, this one must be yours," the older one says to the
little one, holding up the stiff sock that had clung magically to the
mound earlier. They roar with laughter. "Killer socks," the little one
answers. She leans against the bathroom doorway. The hum of the
typewriter distracts her. She hadn't turned it off when she left. "Hy-
dro excessiveness," she chides herself, then shuts it off. *Sun Dogs*, her
new title, stares at her.

"*Sun Dogs*, if you make it, the wallpaper is next."

Tiny Green Waves

Tiny green waves dapple the sea. The diamond-flecked sprigs of sunlight almost seem to compete with the dark layers of green underneath. The waves are so small that it is hard to see the roll between each wave. Not far away, Douglas-firs stand up from the rock and muddy shore and spike the shafts of sunlight, cutting their own green into angled wands of light. Across the mountain bases behind the row of firs, cedars swell. The mountain peaks stretch upward, teasing the clouds as though trying to touch the sky. There doesn't seem to be much valley between the mountains: dark, almost blue-black green is omnipresent. Outsiders, sometimes, feel threatened by the claustrophobic effect of living on a narrow valley floor that is submerged in a bowl whose sides never seem to end, whose dark does not often lighten up, whose green rarely yellows.

To the locals, each hill forms a signpost pointing to some place full of memory. For them, the mountain range demonstrates the smallness of humans. The drama of evergreen mountains reminds them to be modest and yet inspires them to reach for the sky, to be plain and forthright and aggressive about their convictions. I curl up under the view of the mountains, embrace their audacity, the modesty and the incongruity of these spikes that dominate the landscape and yet remain still and calmly lovely.

In the autumn between the stretches of green, the odd gold maple interrupts the landscape. But for that, the green dominates year round. In a way, the accent of maples, almost lost in all that green, only serves to accentuate the dominance of green; it calls to the sameness of it. My eyes close. My mind wanders. The green titillates, moves me, like no other colour can.

From the point at Brighton Park just below the Ironworker's Bridge that binds Vancouver to North Vancouver, I want to relive the riot of fire colours of Vermont in the autumn. Each tree was part of a complex and awesome near-symphony of fire colours. Sumac trees, whose red was so intense and so blood-red pure they didn't seem real, punch through the groves of sugar maple, squeeze themselves between the brilliant unending red, gold, yellow and burnt-orange sugar maple leaves. They have an odd quality about them. It is as if someone has tie-dyed each leaf. The maples on the West Coast are plain by comparison, so oddly dull against Vermont's scarlet maples that I almost forget how much I loved the sight of all those golden polka dots punctuating the green.

Odd that while in Vermont, I think only of the imposition my mountains at home represented, pushing up against chronically grey skies. From the car, I cancel them out and force myself to study the clear blue sky hovering over the extravaganza of colour that Vermont presents on the eve of winter sleep.

Inside the car, voices drift over the joke the Métis present to some Indigenous people. I hear them. The sounds grate against my reality. I am a brown Status Indian; I have a reservation and a nation. I am no longer part of the dispossessed Métis diaspora of relatives whose mothers were Indigenous and whose fathers were white. I am also cognizant that any European blood travelling in the veins of Status Indians likely comes from a white woman or from white men who could not be bothered to marry their Indigenous wives, not from Indigenous women like the Métis. The burgeoning anti-Métis shark-eating frenzy whips up a feminist outrage inside me. I shudder at the anti-Indigenous-woman sentiment underneath the comedy. I am also horrified—the two jokers are women, mixed-blood reservation women.

My mother lies on her deathbed. My fellow women travellers cannot possibly know this; I have declined to tell them. She is dispossessed of community, but her Métis roots show up in the blackness of her eyes, and the way she handles her departure from this world with such grace. The road whips by under spinning wheels that hum an old highway song and every now and then I hear the *kerflup* of the concrete that marks the Americanness of this highway. The *kerflup* runs like a comma between the series of concrete blocks that characterize American roads. Canadian highways are asphalt, not concrete, so there is no *kerflup*, just a mesmerizing hum. We are heading for one of those interminable conferences. The jokes are shredding my insides, but the speakers have no idea that their words scrape at the depths of me.

The driver knows. He stiffens, clamps his mouth shut. His throat constricts like there are claws holding it closed. It locks his voice. His face is aimed straight forward; his eyes focus intently on the road. He neither agrees nor disagrees. At least he declines to participate in the laughter that follows the joke. Perhaps he does not want to engage in a dispute over this, or maybe he refuses to choose sides. I want him to choose sides. I stare at the stunning reds in the landscape swishing by and wonder why I want this.

"Choose me" sounds so elementary, so childish. His choosing sides would be some fantastic show of affection, I tell myself. It wouldn't be. In his refusal to choose, I paint a picture of a shell encasing his heart. The shell hardens, expands to cover his whole body. He needs this encasement. Here it comes, my acid mouth. Keep it shut.

I focus on the trees. Blood red, scarlet red, magenta, fuchsia, gold, yellow, orange and tangerine fight to retain each bit of desperate paled green as each leaf clings to the last second of life. For a brief moment, a crack in the landscape's war against dying lays bare a yellow softened grassy meadow full of vulnerable left-leaning tiger lilies. Maybe there is a crack in his armour, too. Maybe between the maps of hardness on the outside, there is a vulnerable, soft inside. This is likely fiction, but the thought of it softens those hard spaces inside me. Perhaps I prefer fiction.

He is a barracuda. I have settled on that. Barracudas are stealthy, smooth, fast swimmers; quiet, intelligent beings who enjoy the art of killing as much as they enjoy eating their prey. They entrap sharks; turn them into pariahs against themselves, inspire them to some insane state of hysteria. Hysterical sharks spin into a feeding frenzy, with one another as the main course. Not good for the sharks. Sharks are crazy; they look like they are having some kind of an orgasm when they feed on each other. I don't really know that much about sharks. This is an old story, fiction, but I prefer fiction, so I run with it.

Barracuda. I like the sound of it. I remind myself that it's okay to be a barracuda if you don't walk on two legs. A human barracuda is a shell, empty inside, with a stealthy and vicious surface that is driven to predation, to winning at all cost. At any moment, the shell could crack, in fact, the shell is always under threat by the possibility of actually having to shift positions and expose the soft underbelly, or the lack of a shift could expose the hard shell of the barracuda and the emptiness inside. A human barracuda must always plan the next shark frenzy to prevent this. He must always seek new prey, not a single prey, either, but a group, a pod, a whole gang of prey.

I decline to engage him or the two women. I am too raw. I cannot conjure the sort of logic that might lead to some kind of emotional transformation in the women. I could just slam dunk them. That would make me a predator, a barracuda. On the other hand, my silence smacks a little of shark. Barracudas use thought to advance their hold on prey, not to alter their fundamental selves. I refuse to be a barracuda, but I don't like sharks much either.

He grips the steering wheel too tightly. His breathing slows and shallows. I have this reputation for blurting out exactly what I think, disrupting the harmony of unchallenged hypocrisy. Today that won't happen, but he doesn't know this. I am a minnow on my way to the falls. I wait in the shadows for a man who will traverse the rest of the journey with me; I am not concerned that it may not be him who finishes it. Unlike salmon, I am aware that the man I finish the journey with does not have to be the man I began it with, nor will it necessarily be the man who heaves me over the falls. I know it doesn't matter who helps me scale the falls. The point is not who gets there with whom, but that someone returns to the spawning grounds to recreate minnow culture. I have told him this, but he knows that the birth of minnow culture spells death for barracuda ways. He chooses to hold tight to his barracuda shell. It must feel safer.

The gold and red hues of autumn's peaceful acquiescence to death have left his face long ago. The colours don't dance on his cheekbones anymore. Instead, paled grey barracuda smiles emerge as he charms his way into swallowing prey. These grey smiles emerge between feeds and vanish in the clear autumnal light. The emotion inspiring the smile sours in his throat. I can smell the sour. The poetic language of ancestors, whose voices were so incredibly vibrant and filled with colour, dies from want of use. And a new collection of words rolls out, screaming louder than the wind which pulls at the dying leaves, screaming louder than the buried words. The words dissipate, the poet in him perishes, becomes a danger.

One of the women in the back repeats the lines of derision and asks the driver for affirmation. He is still frozen. Both women laugh again. I try to bury my rage in the folds of the trees. Let the wind carry it to its birthplace far away. Bias is not a reasonable thing. It is emotional, conjured by those whose own life is rich with doubt and pain they have no idea what to do with, so they pass it on to those that society has deemed lesser beings. It is a kind of crazy social contract that the colonized have unconsciously agreed to. Bias colours the distance between us, but it need not spawn anger—yet I still feel this nameless, victimless rage burning in my guts. It's a crazy kind of systemic rage I cannot explain to anyone, and it is always looking for someone to land on.

Both these women are my friends. Neither of them is culturally intact. Neither am I, nor is anyone really. But they continue to hold themselves above the "lost Métis" who claim an indigenous self that is contradictory. The lightness of their hair and skin betrays them, but they see no conflict between their derision of mixed bloods not from reserves that Canada has sanctioned as Indian and the reality of their own mixed-blood heritage. They have a reserve. Canada names them Indigenous. They may or may not love this fact, but it has nothing to do with truth. The truth is that their behaviour indicates a crazy reliance on the outside world for the definition of themselves. He knows that I know this.

He fears something, maybe a quarrel. This compelling sense of logic cannot jar his distorted feelings loose from the anchor of pain that holds them in tack. The tendrils of years and years of barracuda behaviour secure the anchor. He would have to tell the truth if I said anything.

I leave the voices. I wonder where the poetry of this land is buried. Is it there in that paled yellow meadow of calm? Or maybe it is in the blood-colour near-dead leaves about to be taken up by a storm-maddened autumn wind. I wonder what the sales pitch style oratory—which cloaks the lost story of ancestors who must have seen these colours, charactered them up, *storied* them and presented life, law, love and philosophy in impossibly beautiful colours— sounded like before barracuda culture set in. The colours interrupt my fiction. They are so beautiful they almost hurt to look at. I want to drift about the stories anew and re-imagine them in the light of this glorious autumn. I want to see the language they must have birthed. I want to feel the old Indigenous speaker's heart beating in my own chest and see the gold and red on the faces of the people. I want to harness the power of this car to some kind of paint machine made of sugar-maple red and repaint the whole world.

The car slows, the landscape alters. We are winding our way through narrow country lanes. The houses hug the edge of the road. They are plain, small and not well-built rez houses, unsubsidized, functional. No one here seems to care much for middle class re- spectability. The conversation shifts. A story is being told. I half listen.

"That's where we burned a bunch of old hoboes." That's where the barracuda first put the sharks into a feeding frenzy.

All over the community there are contending signs: "No Bingo," "Bingo means Development," "Vote for so-and-so from the such-and-such party." I want to know about this multi-party election and the bingo conflict, but the colours of autumn still stain the thoughts in my mind. The trees, their colours are too powerful for me to want to trivialize their effect, as a conversation about political parties and bingo quarrels would do. I spin around the possibility of talking my way back into the trip. They are laughing at the image of burning hoboes rolling around in the grass. It doesn't feel possible to make my way into that, so I don't bother trying. It is not that they were mean. I just feel too deficient to trail through the journey from my imaginary world into the thin mask of reality their inappropriate laughter presents without hurting them.

They are good people, but I have to let my rage simmer to a boil. This kind of rage is dangerous to let loose. The receiver would survive, but their dignity would be forever assaulted. I like them. Their bias isn't all that serious. It isn't hinged to anything valuable. My rage is the kind that demands destruction, or at least ostracism. I don't believe I have the right to unleash it by myself. I am a minnow; we do things en masse, so I remain silent.

Barracudas laugh at the tenderness of minnows. They are mistaken about the tenderness; it is the desire to swim upstream with our brethren, all of us, even the relatives we don't like. We are all going to head upstream together, help one another scale the falls, all in the interest of creation and procreation, no matter how mad we are at each other—this makes us careful how we say things. What the barracudas don't consider is that we are never alone. It takes courage for millions to swim against the tide and the full length of an entire river, to scale series after series of falls for creation, knowing that death waits. The fight is not made for us but for the future. It is not a fight against anything or anyone but rather a fight for creation. We know creation itself is the only winner and we are satisfied, content with this knowledge. We also know that millions of us are vital to this fight.

In the place of peace where his affection is lives a barracuda's desire for more things than he needs. It has replaced his affection for creation. Every day, he pulls in the ways from the outside that deepen his disaffection for creation. Every day, he consumes the rewards that require watching others fall into a feeding frenzy competing with one another over spoils. He thickens the layer of barracuda armour to avert the empathy that would dull his competitive edge. In the end, loneliness is all that is left. He learns to live with it by filling his life with people, acquiring indispensable knowledge and gaining more and more recognition—charm is all it takes.

He thinks no one sees behind the charm. He doesn't know that people are aware he does not believe himself. He doesn't realize some of us see his huge loneliness and hear the tormented scream inside. Not everyone is fooled, but other barracudas buoy up his false face mask. They can use what they see to entrap, and use him. Inadvertently, against his will, he strengthens them against himself.

He knows this possibility exists, it arouses fear in him, but he cannot see the direction it is coming from. Everyone becomes suspect until, so clouded is his vision, he becomes trapped by his own false desires. The grey concrete becomes attractive. Vehicle exhaust smells alright, and the maddened pace of the self-destructive death-culture of the European world looks so good.

He covers his trace by recreating children after his own image. Children who see him as a source of never-ending things and not as a lonely aging man who needs affection. The storm it would take to alter his course is too great. No one would understand. No one would sympathize. He has recreated himself too completely, paying great attention to every detail of the image he constructed. He has bequeathed his barracuda ways to too many of those people who might love him. What loyalty he has garnered, in exchange for things, has been lost. He does not believe nature leaves a vacuum. He believes that any cessation of his barracuda ways would result in the loss of what little loyalty he has acquired. He paid dearly for this loyalty. It cost him his sense of self and the power to love.

We had argued about Métis before. He could not defeat the compelling logic inherent in our culture, but I knew he had not changed his emotions.

I hear voices laced with suspicion and doubt. They wed themselves to threat, the way suspicion and doubt generally do when the threat is unfounded and the doubt absurd. I see the wedding and watch the birth of meanness, the only progeny created when lonely doubt fills the inside hearts of people who have had their gentle ways layered under barracuda culture. These layers scorn the soft velvet leaves of sugar maple and the ways these maples must have inspired in the people of Cattaraugus. In the autumn, the thin shell of barracuda culture obscures the music of the symphony which precedes re-birth and dulls the heart of belief under each layer, until belief itself rages dense and small inside, spelling danger to those who have traded seeing and feeling their way past the doubt for vestments of barracuda ways.

I am weary of the current sound of our voices. Everywhere I go in Indigenous homelands these days, I hear the voice of Emerson and his "basically, basically, basically, fundamentally" Latin influence. I am weary of social engineers and their "designated, designated, designated" whatevers. I am weary of First Nations speakers who refer to their own as "them . . . them . . . them . . . and you guys" as though they were not First Nations people themselves. I am weary of hearing our history recounted in the esoteric rhetoric we can't own. I am weary of hearing that the people Europeans met were "dancing, happy and friendly" as though we had no minds coming from our own mouths. We, who should know better, I am weary of being told these people don't really have an existence except as "imagined communities."

In our original lives, to imagine was to harness the power of ceremonial being and re-create a vision of the world. In our lives, the imagination was of greater significance in the process of being than any current reality. No one in my lineage imagined despots. No one in my lineage imagined genocide of trees, people, stone or anything else. In our original culture, no one could imagine a whole people who did not have the perfect right to be, to enjoy the gifts of life.

In our English, it is the process of conjoining spirit, heart, body and mind that delivers imagination. For us, these people have no imagination. "Imagined communities" is such a pitiful misunderstanding of the process of ceremonial thought. I am weary of our men tripping over the "right of white women to own property" as an injustice and then presenting the ownership of property itself as the root of injustice to earth and all her children. The Western language of sociology, anthropology and just plain salesmanship obscures heart.

I am weary of fighting for a place in the world of Indigenous people. If I said something, likely I would be told that they "consider me Indigenous, not Métis" and my whole lineage's history of betrayal would be trivialized in this way. It would feel like I did when the one white man who expressed an interest in me said, "I consider you white." The trees, their colours are too powerful for me to want to be trivialized. I spin around the possibility of talking my way back to significance in their eyes and changing their minds about Métis. It doesn't look possible, so I don't bother trying. It is not that I feel the women are too biased, but I feel much too deficient of affection for them to trail through the journey from cultural purity to European bias, to make any plausible or believable argument without hurting them.

I am weary of the trace elements of European culture we have woven overtop our own. There is little out there I value. Most of what we have yarned over top our selves is not worth having. That we don't see, stuns me.

I am weary of European theories of stress, pain and peeling back the layers. I know deep inside the heart of every human, seduced by barracuda culture, lives desire —a human desire—a poetic desire for re-birth. I know deep inside myself this cannot be realized without pushing up the whole of Europe and recovering belief. I know this belief is buried dangerously deep, that the upheaval will cost lives that only war—internal war—and a dogged determination to find peace will push up. I know fear pulls humans into the seductive rewards of clinging to a predatory culture.

Inside he feels a thin thread of doubt. It lingers overtop his history. "It isn't enough to see my children each week. We aren't close. I want to talk to them, but am not sure how." The yearning dies with its own inability to be born through the layers of grey predatory ways. It dies in the lap of his deep knowledge that he had recreated these ways in his children. Hope perishes and he returns to the place where the creation of a shark-eating frenzy would settle his deepest desire and push it back to the end of the tunnel where it has always remained hidden. It takes a humble heart to peel away the layers. For barracudas to be barracudas they must cling hard to their arrogant hearts. Paradox.

The sap of the maples runs hot in springtime as long as the weather outside runs cold. In order to heat the blood inside, the outside must be cold. Perhaps he needs to be chilled with loss before his own blood will run hot with compassion. It is overwhelming, this hot sap in a cold context. Perhaps in some strange way the paradox of hot sap against a cold world brings up the blood lust of barracudas, hangs onto it and justifies it.

Perhaps the cling is made of his own beginnings. It cost a life to bring him into the world, his mother's life. It cost him his mother's love, his father's loyalty. In the end, the price of his being was loneliness. Perhaps he believes he is obligated to pay this price. Perhaps it isn't the offerings of barracuda society at all, but this simple beginning: life in exchange for loneliness—lovelessness. The only way for him to pay the price as a man is to retain the essential barracuda ways that layer themselves into a crazy kind of mean protection from love.

The presentation of the legacy of internal colonialism as a road out does not exist for him. Someday he will realize that the trees nourished him, that the wind was a moment of deep realization of life itself, that death is not a negative but a powerful beginning. He will see that the world we desire is a human one. A world rich in colour, alive with affection and absent of massive loneliness. The children of barracudas are already connecting with minnows and the leaves of readying themselves for winter death. In the end, poetic spirit will re-paint the colours on the hearts of his children, despite his disbelief in them.

As I stare into the red, it transforms to some sort of magical mist, as though the leaves were transparent and all that was left was this misty red aura. Through the leaves, a flower-garlanded woman appears floating elegantly ahead of villagers. She appears to be old, hundreds of years old. She smiles through the misty red, and the rage that burns inside me softens. Flowers forever blossoming soften the rage, cool it, my eyes water, underneath the redness of my own rage blooms hope. I close my eyes and the *kerflup*, *hum*, *kerflup* of the wheels overtaking space soothes. I stop wondering at my rage and focus on flowers, on the forever blooming flowers. Seasons come and go like people, like time, like all things big or small, nothing is permanent but this death, this transformation and the flowering.

Cedar Sings

Cedar sings. She stands at the edge of Squamish territory, near Whistler Mountain before it was a ski resort, overlooking Howe Sound. This is the place where you can hear Raven sing, too. Today, the ancestors who people the mountains between North Vancouver and Whistler are dancing—potlatch dancing. If you look close you can see them. They look like sun spots dappling the tips of the wrinkles on the water of the sound. Can you see? No matter. They are there.

Cedar sings the song she hears from the deep. She knows the song. It is not meant for her. It is for the Squamish people who live along the shoreline in the south and nestle among the mountains not far from Whistler. Well, they used to live along the whole shoreline, but now they have but a few villages in a new place called North Vancouver. Cedar has moved well back into the mountains.

Raven can see Cedar having trouble getting anyone to hear her song. Not even the wind whistling through the trees is helping them to hear. Even the loud sounds coming from the bottom of the sea escapes their attention. So she comes up from the deep. Foosh!

"Cut it out. No one's listening." Raven squawks. "Reminds me of all the trouble we went to in the last century. These other people make too much noise for anyone to hear. These others are magnificently frustrating. They have been here for a hundred years, but they behave as though they never left home. Don't know anything about the place and still make so much noise no one can hear themselves think!"

"Don't talk in riddles Raven. Be clear," Cedar sounds fatigued. Singing can be tiring.

"Don't you remember Capilano told Pauline Johnson, the poet, the story of the double-headed sea serpent? She wrote it down. Put it in a book. No one paid attention. They won't pay attention, not now. They are too preoccupied by toys."

"That story was about greed. What's your problem now, Raven?"

(Squawk) "You don't think greed is still a problem?"

Raven is hopping up and down, pacing back and forth on Cedar's branch. Tell the truth. Raven doesn't sound too bad when she sings from the bottom of the sea. But, up here, on land her voice is a little pesky sounding. When she paces across the skin of Cedar's branch like that, the combination of strident voice and feet scratching on Cedar's skin is unbearable.

"Be calm," Cedar admonishes.

"Everybody wants everything calm nowadays. Take a look. They want things they don't need. How can I be calm? What's worse, no one sings anymore—they buy stereo systems to sing for them. What kind of nonsense is that? They don't tell stories anymore—they sit in front of the TV and let it tell them stories. They are all down there right now, Indian chiefs, politicians, people all arguing about how much each is going to get from the other, who gets to control the remote or some other such nonsense. Land, water, fish, timber is all up for grabs and the people just stay glued to their TV's and stereos as though all was right with the world."

Cedar sighs. She can see Raven's anger is going to get in the way of good sense if she doesn't settle down as anger does sometimes. "The Indians want all that stuff from other people because the government took the original stuff away. The people really only want what is theirs."

Raven squawks, "Theirs—theirs—theirs." The wind blows. Cedar's hair gets tangled and her branches nearly fall off.

"Theirs— are the plastics theirs, the electronics? No. What's theirs is the fruit of the land, the bounty of the sea for survival, not the baubles them others made. They're carving up the land. The people and their politicians are arguing over it like it really belongs to them. You, Cedar should know better. You are barely more than a child, where are all your Elders? Dead. Where are the little babies? Gone. Your past and your future have been traded for an iPod. You are in danger and you can't run away."

Cedar shivers. The wind blows more violently and a branch snaps. It lands on one of Cedar's saplings below, crushing the life out of her child. She weeps.

We sing.

She weeps, but no one hears.

Raven feels remorse pass through her crusty personality. It makes her feel a little pouty.

"Listen to me. You always want to argue with me." Raven sits still on Cedar's branch until Cedar stops crying.

Cedar sees Raven's face change. She looks desperate. Cedar considers Raven's desperation carefully. Cedar knows when someone is desperate she must give them what they want. What does Raven want? Can she give it to her? Peace maybe. Cedar decides not to aggravate Raven anymore. It is as much peace as she could give. Relax and listen. Cedar fishes for some piece of Raven's words that she might want to know more about. "What do you mean traded for an iPod?"

"Clear-cutting, selling the cuts, buying toys, iPods. It's murder—genocide—that's what they're up to now."

"Indians wouldn't do that. They don't log that way. They used horses and culled out the big ones leaving the babies behind."

"That was 1960, the decade in which everything changed. This is the new millennium and no Indian would be caught dead driving a horse."

Cedar shivers again.

Raven reminds Cedar of her history with the others. Thirty years passed and the mountains of the West Coast were skinned. At Wood Fiber, Franklin River, Skidegate and Gitsksan, funeral pyres burned brush, saplings and undersized logs. Drought plagued the rain forests of the West Coast where it rains two hundred inches a year. The rain pulled the earth from the mountains and sent it out to sea. Through it all you screamed and cried but no one heard. What could not be used was burnt. Four fires, mountains high burned constantly for thirty years all along the West Coast and on Vancouver Island. Coast Salish territory's roads were straightened out so that huge trucks could haul out the logs by the millions. And they are going to do it again, straighten out the Sea to Sky highway, only this time some of the people are on their side.

"How are they going to straighten out the road?" Cedar asks as though it mattered.

"Dynamite. They are going to blow up the mountains to fill the ravines."

"Dynamite?" The wind continues to blow and Cedar sways to its rhythm, while Raven continues to persuade Cedar to feel the same desperation that so disturbs her.

"Blow up mountains? Throw them into ravines? Raven, don't exaggerate. There are twenty-seven mountains on this road between here and the city," Cedar objects.

"They can't possibly be thinking about doing that."

"Yeah, that is exactly what they want to do."

"The Salish people would never do that."

"No, but the majority will allow it for a piece of the action. They'll sit in their houses glued to new radios or TV's and let those people do whatever they want to those mountains. Some will even help for a little bit of the action at the Olympic gates."

You can see the Indians in their houses listening to the radio and watching TV and speaking to no one. Raven flies by, sits at the odd window sometimes squawking and objecting. Once in a while, when she thinks no one is looking, she watches a little TV. Who can resist, it is shiny, lovely, awake and dramatic? Raven cannot resist anything shiny.

She is watching Discovery Channel inside someone's house while they were away and hears about this crazy white man who had built an amplifier so powerful you could hear plants talk. The white man was shocked to discover that plants made sound. "Hah, the people knew that before they started listening to you."

"When you make soft sounds, the plants coo; when you yell, they scream," and he gave it a demonstration. "The plant begins to die if you keep yelling at it."

"Idiot, of course they do; they're just like people."

The arrogant white man continued by stating surprise that plants must be emotional beings. Raven tries not to laugh.

"What do you think emotions are made of blood, bone? Where do you think they live, in your head? Try having a feeling in your brain. Pah!" She flies off.

When night falls, Raven sits on a wire outside the house window where she had been watching the TV. She is feeling a bit guilty and she can't get the amplifier out of her head. Somehow this machine is very important to her. Finally, Raven devises a plan.

Off the wire and off to the mountains she flies. She dives into the water and comes up from the deep. She sings to the few remaining giant cedars. This is at Opitsit—near Tofino on the west coast of Vancouver Island.

"Did you know Old Woman—some white guy has gone and invented a machine that can amplify sound thousands of times? He wired it up to some plants. They can hear the sounds they make. The silly things are surprised that when plants are happy they coo; when they are sad they cry." Cedar laughes.

"So, what's your point?" Cedar is getting a little cynical and testy by now. She barely escaped genocide, but for the Elders of Opitsit, who organized a bunch of youth to stop the murder of the Elders.

"Imagine if we could get a hold of that machine and wire it up to the forest the loggers were cutting. The Indians would hear it for sure. The white men might even hear it. They'd come out of the bush, out of their houses and tell them to quit. Imagine their stereos amplifying the screams of a forest of cedar. It would drive them crazy and the loggers would run out of the bush screaming in terror—you know?"

"You want that we should go get the machine? Remember, I can't move."

"I want that you should help me to shape shift into a giant man, and I will go and get the machine."

Cedar agrees to help. They think at first, that maybe they can get Raven to the mainland in a big canoe, but Raven isn't keen on stealing from the Indians. They don't like that idea. In the end, they decide that Raven will ride a truck to town as a crow and then shape shift when she gets to where the machine is and grab it. Then load it onto the truck, shape shift and drive the truck back and bring it to the forest.

When Raven arrives in the town, it takes a little trouble to get the machine out. As you know white guys treat their machines as if they were sacred. Their bosses hire men to guard their sacred objects. The men are armed. But Raven is an astute shape shifter. She changes herself to look like anything or anyone. She changes herself into the boss's shape and orders the men to load the machine onto the truck and then she hauls it first to Haida Gwaii where Guujaaw heard the screaming. Then she takes it to Opitsit where Columpa hears it, and then to Gitksan where Jean hears it. It is too late to do much for poor Squamish, no big trees left there.

All hell breaks loose. Every Indian faller hears it. They run about the forest hysterical. They quit their jobs, block the roads to stop logging. Soon they start singing, feasting, and potlatching. White men keep logging after the Indians block the road, even a few tone-deaf Indians keep logging. Some of the loggers want to run over the Indian protesters. They are mad. The police are called. What right did the People have to threaten the loggers' pay cheques? Police arrest the People. Soon they are going to jail. Old ladies, children, men, women, they are all arrested and sent to jail. Most of the children and old ladies have never been to jail. They are surprised that the guards feed them and the cell has a small bed which gives them time to rest, so they don't mind. Some white man promised to negotiate and the people are relieved. No more jail for their Elders. In court, the judge agrees to stop the logging until the whole mess is sorted out.

"But they haven't won a case yet," Cedar points out after listening to Raven tell the story of the day she drove the loggers out of the forest.

"The point, Cedar, was to get the people out of the house and talking to those other people," Raven answers smugly.

"Oh," Cedar sighs. It is Raven's point, not hers. Her point is to stop the clear cut; Raven's is to alter the direction of relationships between the people and other living beings. Cedar supposes that in the end, this might solve the problem for her grandchildren, but likely it will be too late for her.

On the next storm wind that blew, Cedar lies down and surrenders to her fate.

Scarlet Requiem

From the window, scarlet leaves danced. The air outside crunched cold against the pane inside. The coolness drifted over the top of the vinyl cover on the back of the home-made bench he kneeled on. He could feel it. It pricked at his nose whenever he pressed it up between the wooden bars that separated the panes of glass. His warm breath against the cool air was vaporous. It clouded his view. It misted the dancing leaves. He could still hear them though, slipping, sliding and whistling their way through their last song before winter put them all to rest on the earth below. No one else in the room paid any attention to the leaves. He turned to look in the direction of the murmuring voices. Through a large doorway he could see his aunts leaning forward intently and whispering. The men in the room didn't seem to have anything to do with the kitchen table conversation. Most of them hovered about the old McLary stove or leaned against a doorway or wall. Some of them smoked quietly. One of them sat in a corner of the room Paulie was in; his elbows rested on his knees while his eyes let go a steady stream of tears, but he made no sound. Paulie couldn't figure out why neither the dying leaves nor he called anyone to attention. He wasn't sure why this moment was eerie, maybe scary, but he was sure it was. A single leaf cut loose from the herd above eye level. It made him start. He jumped away from the window. Like the people in the room, its movement was erratic and urgent looking.

Bits and pieces of words floated around him. They followed the movement of more leaves. These words didn't seem to have much

to do with him. Every now and then some tearful woman picked
him up, held him, shed a few tears and then deposited him back at
the window pane. He accepted these hugs without response, and
then he resumed his death watch over the sugar maples in the yard.
The noise today was unusual, uncomfortable. Maybe it wasn't loud
enough. He didn't know what it was, but it was wrong. Besides,
there were too many people in the room.

Death's usual reverence was uncomfortable for these women
who looked forward to life. The death of Paulie's mom didn't inspire
reverence. She was too young. He heard his one aunt whisper that
it was obscene for her to leave so soon. Fearful resignation settled in
on the faces of the women who needed death's reverence to feel comfortable, hopeful. The murmurs were steady, the sounds all muffled,
the meaning unclear. He turned to look at the moving figures, all
large, all just a little edgy. Nothing was smooth. Everyone spoke in
soft low tones, but their bodies couldn't lie. They didn't look soft,
jerking about stiffly as they were and weeping every time they caught
sight of him. The stiffness, the tears and the unsuccessful fight for
reverence scared him. He returned to the view outside. His hands
pressed against the sill's edge with grim determination. His knuckles
whitened slightly under the tan brown fingers. He had no name for
this change in colour. No name for the murmuring bustle behind
him. No name for the sound of the wind through the sugar maple or
the whispering of leaf after leaf as the wind tore them from the tree.
The tree mothered these leaves; he could feel this motherhood and he
tried to wonder why she cast them off in the cold wind, but no words
took shape in his mind—just feelings.

Feelings of dread, feelings of cold, violent feelings, grew inside
Paulie as the hustle and bustle of people who failed to find reverence intensified, and they grew stiffer and stiffer with the effort. Sad
feelings mingled with cold air and the foggy vapour of his breath,
clouded the riot of names for the colours and deepened his sadness.
He had no idea why.

One of the men, his daddy, sat tense in his chair. He said nothing. He never looked at Paulie. Every now and then, one of the other men would touch his shoulder, but the man never moved. All day he sat and stared as he drank cup after cup of coffee. The sound of him sipping coffee seemed to intensify his morose silence.

There was a shift in the tension in the room behind him. He started. It made him want to guard his back. The voices became crisper, more definitive. Each woman took turns laying out the situation as she saw it. His name came up every now and then. He cringed at its mention in the context of the unfamiliar language and unknown decision-making. The old woman in the corner changed his name. He didn't recognize this new name, so he thought they had stopped talking about him and he resumed his own death watch over autumn. A wet rag suddenly landed on him from his right side. He wasn't ready for it. It scraped at his face. He twisted; a hand clutched the top of his head and held him still. No sense struggling; the hand was too big, too determined.

"Hold still now." She cleaned the tears and mucus from his face. The edge in her voice was new. A ball of hot sound swam up from his chest to his face. He was about to let it go.

"Don't cry now," she cajoled softly, almost sweetly, and he stopped, confused. *Don't cry now?* These words were new; Mommy never said them. A dark whirl set itself in motion in his mind. A whirl of movement, images of some other time he couldn't define. No names for days, nights, weeks—just a generic sense of before,— before, it was okay to cry, before, there weren't all these people here, just Mommy, Daddy and Paulie. Paulie, the name glided about, shrank and grew small and distant.

Panic. He felt it. It was a memory so close to now. Mommy, something happened to Mommy, and in the whirl of images a moment was held, smoky-looking and unclear, but very still. In this moment, Mommy was near the door trying to leave. She didn't look quite right. She leaned against it, slid down the length of its frame and then collapsed. Above her Paulie could see a spider drop toward her. It hung ominously by a single silken thread. She looked so big and so small at the same time. Slowly the spider drifted toward her. It threatened to land on her face. He turned away and caught sight of the view behind him of leaves falling helplessly to the ground. He panicked. Screams came from somewhere inside of him, so foreign-sounding and full of terror that he wasn't sure who it was that screamed. He ran toward her and grabbed her dress. A hand moved to get him out of the way. The hand jerked at the little boy who could still hear the scream. Another pair of hands pried the boy's fingers loose and the big hand tossed him aside. The images in the room grew fuzzy. Paulie could see a little boy crouched in the corner, mouth open and no sound coming out, but he was too unfamiliar with his own face to know it was him. At the recollection of this memory his hand clutched the sill. He tried to help his mind hold onto the memory. It felt important to hold the memory still, to look at it, but it slipped far away into a dark tunnel where it seemed to have come from.

A decision was made, a decision he had no name for. The feeling of its finality set in. The women rose and began removing things from the shelf. Paulie's hand went up. He reached in the direction of the women who took Mommy's things and put them in boxes. No one paid attention to his hand. What had they decided? The nameless presence of their decision and their current actions overwhelmed him. The panic rose again, grew intense. It rested in the centre of the finality which took up all the space but for the small piece of his panic. The finality gained weight. It pressed up against the small boy, pushed him closer to the wall. He could hardly hold his head up. His eyes looked at the floor. He pushed back on the finality. His panic subsided. Push back. It settled the insides to push back.

"Tony—Paulie—Get away from the window." The young woman reached for him. He didn't move. Push back. Hold the sill. Watch the leaves. Let the room have its movement, its scary rhythm, its finality. Paulie will stay put. She couldn't move him by herself.

Soon another set of hands helped to loosen his grip and the other swung him upward. He froze. "You're not my mom." It came out rich with threat, full of push back, but the room only laughed at its venom. The body of the boy was too small to carry out the threat that laced his voice. They knew it and found his words amusing. He knew it too, but it felt good to say it. She held him up, smiled. Paulie didn't smile back. He glared, just for a moment, then pushed that down inside. It whirled delicately inside—a tiny leaf of red emotion he cast downward to some place deep within his body. It whistled a high-pitched scream only Paulie heard as it floated and landed with a quiet whisper inside him. His eyebrows rose, almost skeptically so; his eyes grew dark, full of threat; it scared the woman and she stopped. He was aware he had scared her. He made her put him down with just a look—a cold, intense look. He felt power surge inside as he ended his aunt's intrusion this simply.

Paulie tasted this moment of power. He grabbed hold of it hard. He practised all day until dark dropped over him. He would have forgotten about it, but the next day bloomed the same as the one before...the window, the sugar maple tossing off her leaves, the bustle, the stiff bodies and their incongruously quiet tense voices and, eventually, the finality of another decision made, confusing him again, and then the panic that followed. The pushing back rose of its own accord this time. It came without the need for memory to call it back to life. It came over and over, each time the moment of decision brought the feeling of finality to the room. The colder Paulie's push, the more effect it had on the women around him and the power he felt. His cold glare always ended any unwanted intrusion on his person. It changed the way people spoke to him. Sometimes it even altered the way they moved around the room. At first it didn't seem to permanently discourage them; they all took turns trying to solicit some sort of happy response from him. Each by turn, however, was unnerved by the intensity of his cold glare. Finally they all gave up.

By the third day he became familiar with the sound of the words *Aunt* and *Uncle*. He already knew his Gramma's and Grampa's names. Other words came up that took on familiarity with the repetition of them: *Funeral, Ceremony, After the funeral, After the ceremony*. Finally, his mommy returned. He giggled and laughed triumphantly when they wheeled her in on the same bed that had taken her away. He knew she would be back. She was sleeping. He made a dash for her. He leaped straight from the bench and landed on the wheeled bed. His hands grabbed her dress and he screamed, "Wake up, Mommy!" Voices barked, hands went out and he rose in the air again.

"Get away from there," and he felt panic. His scream died in his throat; it moved outside to where the leaves hurled themselves at the earth. What have they done to Mommy? His tongue moved about in his head, searching for the shape of the words. He knew these words, "What have they done to Mommy?" He looked at the gurney, mouth open, eyes wide and let his panic seize him. His skin grew tight. His muscles pressed against his bones inside. His skin grew tighter, still. His lungs let go of all their air. Everything was so tight, no air wanted to go back inside. His shoulders hunkered down and his hands formed fists. A knot formed in his gut.

He turned his head one last time to look at his mom. She lay so completely still. She was so still, she looked small, frail, despite her weight. The hands carried him past lines of people: aunts, uncles, older cousins. They reached for his cheek, looked shyly sympathetic at him. Underneath the sympathy, there lay the tightened musculature of faces who struggled from some form of nameless control. Paulie did not believe in the nameless surface of sympathy. He saw the tightness behind the faces. He believed the tightness. He felt it inside himself. Tightness is cold, stiff, like the old sugar maple scattering her leaves all over the place.

One by one, the people all left the house. The man with the huge hands went with the gurney. Paulie stopped his own breath as he watched his daddy take his mommy away. This phantom that came home every weekend and disappeared for most of the time was almost unknown to Paulie. Paulie didn't want his dad to take his mommy away. He couldn't find the words to object, and they left.

Paulie had to stay. Funerals were not for toddlers. He lay on the couch, eyes vacant; he stared at the ceiling for a long time, while the young aunt who had volunteered to stay behind with him read stories aloud. She was well-meaning. She wanted to take his mind off the morbidity of his mother's funeral. From the couch, Paulie could still see out the window. Below the drone of his aunt's voice, he thought he could hear the sugar maple scream at the leaves, "Get away from there . . . get away from there . . . get away." The sad sound of it invaded him in some far-away place he was unfamiliar with. It was too far away to make him cry.

He lay so still his aunt worried. She chucked his chin and tried to get some sort of response from him to no avail. He lay there as still as his mom had. It unnerved her. She began to read too fast; her voice got squeaky and went up a pitch higher than usual. She argued this fear into a perverse attachment of blame to Paulie. "Paulie's stubborn. Paulie's spoiled." This helped her voice lose its own fear. The others had said something like this earlier whenever he glared at them, so she saw nothing wrong with her line of reasoning. She didn't recover her empathy for him. The fear gone, her tone took on the finality that Paulie now loathed.

The story lost all joy for Paulie. A hazy image of a woman, book in hand, rose above the sound of the woman's voice. There were smiles all over her face, even her hands seemed to smile as she reached for Paulie. Her image tried to rise above the picture of the screaming scarlet leaves. He could see her mouth move, but her words failed to erase the sound of the leaves who pleaded for their lives. He tried to bury the sound of screaming leaves so that he could hear his mommy. The screaming would not go away. Mommy's soft voice could not drown the screams, until the image of her lost the fight and the screaming leaves wept. A lone tear hid behind Paulie's eyes. It tried to escape but failed. For a brief moment Paulie felt sorry for the leaves. His hand went up in the air as though to reach out and comfort them. They were too far away. His hand hung suspended for a second, then fell helplessly to his side. He tried to remember the leaves, the woman and the sound of Mommy, to hold the images still, but they slipped away.

In the days and weeks that followed people disappeared except for the occasional visit by one or two of them at a time. Paulie and Gramma moved to her house. Paulie didn't care much for the women who came unless they brought other children with them. The women tended to behave as though he was their personal toy. Gramma used these moments of visitation to complain about him, called him a handful, and the aunt who was visiting always supported her by bawling Paulie out. Big fat fingers were shaken at him for things he couldn't remember doing. During these times, Paulie learned to be inconspicuous. As an aunt arrived, he retreated to some corner and busied himself at nothing.

Mostly, the house was empty. It felt lonely. There was a deep sadness all about the house. It filled every room. He stopped looking out the window so much. It didn't seem to help. The feeling of sadness grew almost uncomfortable compared to the wasted hope that lay in searching the window for the return of something he could no longer define.

Daddy came by once in a while in the beginning. He had grown morose and Paulie came to dread his arrival. At the same time, he hoped for an end to his dad's moroseness. He behaved better when his dad came. Maybe this would encourage Dad to be happier. It didn't, and slowly Paulie gave up.

He began to forget Mommy. The images of her grew hazier; they came less frequently and within months they all died. At first he fought for them. Finally he stopped trying to drag the memories up. They were too vague and it tired him to do it. Instead he moved about his Gramma's house and searched for familiarity in the lines of his new home. Eventually the walls took on ordinariness. The rooms became old friends. The sadness and the loneliness became a familiar ambiance that Paulie identified with. The different smells Gramma made when she cooked grew welcome. Fed, he felt some comfort, but most of the time only cold curiosity governed his heart.

Today, the earth turned white. He stared out the window and wistfully watched its whitening. He loved the whitening of each leafless branch. Leafless, the trees lost their scream, and the white was so softly melancholy, like himself, that it was almost a comfort. He watched for something else, too. He couldn't quite remember what it was he looked for—Maybe Daddy— Maybe some unnameable feeling.

Winter perished. Spring came and went, and then summer took its turn. He matured some. He grew old enough to resent not being allowed to go outside on his own, but he accepted his confinement to the house as part of his general condition of estrangement and sadness.

Daddy doesn't live here. He came to this realization some time after hot summer days dwindled into cool mornings. The leaves outside began to orchestrate their death requiem. His visits to the window grew rarer with the intensification of reds over receding green.

Paulie couldn't remember the precise moment he saw it coming. Days merged into other days; memories layered themselves one on top of the other in some crazy fashion like leaves piled one upon the other, suffocating what lay beneath. Then, suddenly, it became clear to him that Daddy wasn't coming back. For some reason Paulie took to wishing for his return. There was a reason for this wish beyond his daddy's return, but Paulie could not remember what it was. The moment it was clear he wasn't coming back, Paulie renewed his vigil at the window and stared at it. He stared out the window a lot. He waited for his dad. His dad was somehow connected to memories he couldn't bring up. He couldn't figure out why but he desperately wanted him to come back. He felt the desperation. Inside his mind he whispered *Daddy* with huge intensity as though to will his return. It didn't seem to matter how often he called him or how hard. Daddy never came back. Deep shame at this failure to recall his father paralyzed him for a long time. He became listless, withdrew into the world of immediate reality around him and buried the world of whirling emotions inside, far from the compelling moments of the here and now. Finally, the words took shape. He had to wait a long time before their intensity subsided enough for him to dare ask his Gramma.

"Gramma, Daddy doesn't live here no more?" he asked one day at breakfast. His voice remained nonchalant as he waited for the answer. He pushed hard at the sound of desperation that threatened to invade his voice. He pushed it back to where it now lived permanently wrapped up in a tiny scream far from his mouth.

"No," she harrumphed. "Now eat your breakfast." Paulie ate in dreadful silence. Outside, the leaves began anew their terrible ceremony. The wind blew and the sugar maple shook all her children mercilessly in the wind. Inside, Paulie stared apathetically at the sugar maple shaking off her leaves and decided it was better to be the wind than the trees. He took a bite from his toast and swallowed. He didn't remember that once he had felt so sorry for them all.

The Canoe

Our house is located about 1,000 yards from the ocean on the West Coast of Vancouver Island. A little salt-water lagoon stretches out from behind a row of cedar trees bent away from the wind that almost blocks my view of the sea, but I can still see it. The soft swish of the steady surf drifts up around my ears. It soothes, stills my thinking a little. The gulls are screeching to one another from the shell-draped sandy edges of the lagoon, and off in the distance, I can see seals playing about in the water near the western side of the land just beyond the lagoon. The lagoon is salt water enclosed by land when the tide is out and open to the sea when it is in. A family of swans lives in it for part of the year; the young one ought to be learning to fly soon, but the parents don't seem too concerned or anxious about it. The sun overhead is shining, lighting the tips of the surf diamond-bright as they roll forward. There are a few fluffy clouds in the sky, not enough to threaten rain. The wind coming off the sea cools the skin; it is soft and comforting. I can use a little comfort.

Our house isn't like the ones in town. It is a five-room cabin sporting a simple living room, dining room and big kitchen with two small bedrooms and a bathroom near the back exit. There is no basement, just a crawl space. Out here under the onslaught of salt-sea winds and rain, our car has to be parked in the garage so it doesn't get salt damaged. Unlike some town folks, we don't use it for storage. All the stuff we don't use anymore is stored in a shed. In the front of the house, facing the sea, is a porch as long as the house is wide that my dad built for my mom. There is a swing on it, a two-seater. Dad built that, too. I'm in it. Dad never is anymore. Mom and he used to swing on it before she died about a year ago. They spent their summer evenings rocking back and forth in it, her knitting and him reading the Band mail out loud to her. That's my dad: builds a romantic swing for the love of his life and all he ever did in it was read the Band mail. From the porch, I look out onto the water and wish I wasn't wound up so tight.

My dad is in the old shed. I can hear him from the porch rummaging around. I imagine him shifting things about, maybe ordering things up, and cleaning it out because he wants to start a new project. "Not likely, Jordan," I tell myself. He hasn't started a new project since I was ten years old. Every now and then, the sound of planks hitting the sod floor with a thud reaches me, and I wonder what the heck he is doing in there. To find out, I would have to go there and see, but I hesitate. Another thud followed by a curse. I get halfway up, but something has my feet nailed to the floor of the porch, and so I sit back down and rock the swing.

Lately, things haven't been going so good between us. A quiet, strange and cumbersome time has us both trapped. It's not an easy quiet; it feels thick damp, like some invisible and porous object separates us. The quiet is physical, powerful and at the same time it feels so fragile, like some moment could pop it all, but neither of us knows how to conjure the moment, so we sidestep each other, barely look at one another as we pass by. Every morning I get up and promise myself: today I am going to look him straight in the eye and say something. But I can't figure out what yet. I know the quiet that traps us is connected to our missing my mom. I want to say something profound that will break the silence for him, but when I think of her gone, only little things come up like missing the soft swish swish of her skirt as she moves about the house. I can't just up and tell him that. I miss her smile when I catch her studying me. It seems meager to say that I would give anything to wake up and hear the quiet rattle coming from the kitchen as she cooks.

Her movements were deliberate and austere, thrifty even. Sometimes she paused, leaned away from the cupboard, and lifted her index finger to her cheek, her eyes studying the seasonings above her as she decided what she needed to brighten the meal she had planned for us. Her absence is so huge. But when I try to name it, it comes out all small and petty because I miss those small moments: the way she cupped her cheek and leaned in listening to me, and the pause, the pregnancy of it before she spoke and turned what I said into something more. If I say stuff like that to Dad, it would make her death feel so frail, wispy and trivial.

Another loud bang comes from the shed and my dad hollers. I jump up, but my feet won't move. He must be hurt; maybe something heavy fell on him. And then I hear the sound of glass shattering and my dad lets go a delicious string of urgent curses. I bolt for the shed. By the time I get to the entrance, he is lurching through the door towing the old canoe that sat up on the rafters of the shed for longer than I have been alive. There doesn't appear to be anything wrong with him, but the canoe looks like it could use a little tender loving care. Apparently, on its way down, the canoe fell through an old window, but the glass missed Dad.

"Hey," he pumps out like he has done something he is proud of and I ought to commend him for. My teeth grind a little. I'm trying not to be too mad about the false alarm, and I fight the embarrassment of overreacting to his cussing.

"Hey what?" The sarcasm in my voice is born of a year of resentment. Dad ignores it. He keeps smiling. He hasn't smiled for a while. He looks good for a change.

"Geez, don't throw water at his fire, it isn't going to help. Can't I, just this once, let him have it, let him think I am happy about whatever he is proud of?" Dummy, I just said that out loud. It is out there and I can't take it back, so I do the Indian thing, just pretend I didn't say anything. He does too.

"I thought we'd have a look at this old tub, see if she still floats. If she does, maybe we can take a ride?"

I swallow. And if it leaks? It will be one more thing you can be disappointed about, Dad, one more reason to head for town, grab a bottle of Captain Morgan's and drown yourself in it. I let out the air I am holding in my lungs with a loud sigh. It is a relieving sigh.

"Give me a hand, boy?" He ignores my sigh as well.

The canoe was built by Dad's granddad. It is so old the cedar is a pale grey on the ridges of the wood grain while the valleys are dark, near black. Great Grandpa carved it during the cultural prohibition days, so he did his best to make it look like a giant skiff with no paint and no Indian designs on it like you see on canoes these days. As a skiff, our dugout is plain ugly. Doesn't sound like a great idea to test it while the surf is up, but I can't bring myself to be the reason for Dad's disappointment, so I swing around to the other side and drop back a little distance and pick up the canoe.

We raise her up to our thighs and head to sea, trying not to scrape the bottom on the rocks that dot the land before the sandy edge of shoreline. The tide is partway out, and the bared mudflats are covered in seaweed and kelp. This makes the walk to the sea comic; we slip and slide around. We teeter and totter forward nearly dropping the canoe with every step. I look around to see if anyone is watching. Thank God, everyone went to town. Dad hasn't done this for a while, and I have never done this before, so we are not as steady on our feet as we need to be, but neither of us seems to be able to stop. We stagger, slip, slide, recover our balance and stagger some more toward the sea. With every slip-slide, I convince myself that this is the dumbest thing we have ever decided to do, to test out a shabby, hundred-year-old half-skiff-shaped canoe with a six-foot surf up, but I keep putting one foot in front of the other like my brain has just up and left, and all that's left is the good feeling between us that has never been there before.

"We really should pitch it first, but there isn't any sense doing that unless we know she is seaworthy. Right?" He wants me to agree, so I do, smiling, stupidly. He looks so damn happy. It is so contagious. My knees quiver with fear, but I smile because part of me is having a blast. I can't stop thinking about how truly dumb this is, dangerous even, and at the same time there is a butterfly of joy bubbling around in my belly and I can't stop hauling this tub to the sea. There is no one around to make sure we get back to shore if it isn't seaworthy. Even with his back turned, Dad looks so warm, like the damp quiet cylinder he was trapped in just evaporated and it is melting mine. This is the first time I feel this good doing something with my dad, and even if it is the dumbest thing to do, my feet and arms commit to do it.

Things weren't all that great between us even when Mom was alive. He always talked about me to her even when I was right there in front of him: "Your son needs to learn to fish" or "Your son needs to learn to mow the lawn." Then she would negotiate with me that it was time to learn, and she would send me out with the "wall of silence" that he was. From the day I learned something new, it became a personal chore. Sometimes he was there with me raking while I mowed, or gutting fish I caught, but we never were truly together. I was her son, not his. Mom tried to bridge the distance between us to soften the space, but she was never successful. After her death, there didn't seem any way to heal the rift.

Dad has been moping silently since she died. He looks so old and lost without her, like she had made everything, even me, seem worth his while. So when my cousin Joey suggested a few weeks ago going down to the S-turns, I jumped at the chance. I wanted to blind myself from seeing her. It seemed a better idea than rattling off some list of things I miss and ruining my memory of her.

He caught me. I was drunk as a skunk when I heard the old pickup truck park and saw him jump out and head for me, lips pulled so tight I couldn't see them—and he has very big square Indian lips. He hollered so loud I half sobered up. He grabbed me by the scruff of the neck and dragged me to the pickup. He threw me in the back so hard, I scraped my elbow and tore my jacket. As he sped away from the turns, he kicked up a cloud of dust. He drove so fast I bounced around in the back, thinking any minute I would fly out of the truck. I grabbed the rings on the toolbox bolted to the floor and hung on so tight my skin burned. When he pulled up to the house, he slammed on the brakes. I flew forward and hit my head on the front of the pickup box.

Mercilessly, he strode around to the back and dragged me out of the pickup by the feet, paying no attention to my bleeding head though I knew it wasn't all that serious. He shoved me several times toward the front door; I staggered and fought to keep upright. He didn't say a word. The longer his quiet lasted, the more scared I became. Inside, he poured a tall glass of water and added a tablespoon of salt to it. I wanted to cry for Mom. I wanted to sink into a chair, put my head in my hands and weep. I prayed for my dead grandma to come get me; I prayed for my mom to come and get me, for the floor to swallow me, even for lightning to strike me, but no one came except Dad and nothing happened except for the jar of salt water he held in his hand.

He handed it to me and ordered me to drink. I drank. I vomited. He ordered me to drink more. I threw up half the night. I heard him say, "Have another drink, you fool." I did, and then I vomited some more. The next day he kicked the end of my bed. "Get up!" I scrambled into my jeans, tossed my shirt on and jumped into my sneakers in one heck of a hurry. This shameful feeling of wanting to do anything to please him swept through me, just so he would calm down and stop being so angry.

"Get in the truck." The look on his face scared me more now that I was sober. He was madder than I had ever seen him. My dad has always been a crusty man with a short fuse, but I got used to that early. The crustiness was never this furious. My mom on the other hand was always soft and reasonable. She acted like she wondered why I did things, then she'd ask what I was thinking, like she seriously wanted to know. When I told her, she would ask if I thought I'd achieved my goal. Now my legs were shaking so hard I could hardly walk. I fought the urge to wet my pants. Dad's eyes stayed cold and furious as he drove the pickup across the reserve.

He stopped at the S-turns and my heart sank. What is he going to do to me? He handed me a garbage bag. Through his teeth he growled out, "Clean it up!"

Clean it up? At first I was relieved, but then I took a look around. The S-turns were an incredible mess, years of teenage party filth and memorabilia lay everywhere. Garbage is repulsive. I really didn't want to do this. I did not make this mess by myself. Some of the garbage was so old I pictured my dad creating it. It wasn't fair. I looked up to say something and saw his face. It was hateful. I dared not argue with him. I felt so alone and so bitterly lonely. I realized, for the first time, that I was always going to be a motherless child. He sat in the truck while I picked up every old paper wrapping, pop can, beer can and cigarette butt until the bag was full. I tossed the bag into the truck, and then I saw his arm hang out the window. In his hand was another bag. The sun beat down on me, the sweat poured out of me, and I faced my first hangover, picking up the dirtiest bunch of garbage imaginable, wondering if I was going to make it to manhood. After a while, I succumbed to the work at hand. I challenged myself to be thorough, to be quick and careful.

After I filled four bags, I stood beside the box of the pickup waiting for whatever to come next. Dad signaled me to get in beside him. I did not want to get in next to him, to sit next to all that hate and rage, but the need to please was bigger than my resistance, so I got in. I sat up as straight as I could. If I didn't feel brave, at least I could look the part. Dad looked out the window on his side. He stared out the window without starting the truck for a few seconds.

"Son, I am no good at this parenting stuff. Your momma always took care of that. She," his voice cracked. I fought back a sob I dared not let go because underneath it were more sobs, big wracking ones; I swallowed hard to push the sob down. Don't cry Dad, please don't do that. "I am damned sure she didn't want you hanging out drunk by the S-turns. She wanted better things for you." He leaned onto the steering wheel, then his head dropped onto his arms and he moved his head from side to side like a half-blind big old bear trying to see something.

"I'll try to get better at parenting, but you have to find in yourself the desire never to violate her memory." He sat up, put the keys into the ignition, turned the engine over and slowly drove away. The hate in his eyes melted.

That was a month ago. After that, things got real rugged between us and we had no one to soften it. Since then, he has just walked sad and silent. That didn't feel any better than his rage, though it did melt my desire to please him a little. I definitely did not want to join Joey and the others by the S-turns, not so much for fear of Dad but out of respect for Mom. He was right: she wanted more for me, and even if I didn't feel like I wanted more for myself, right now, I should at least fake it until I do. I was beginning to feel alright when Dad got the idea to drag out the old canoe. I talked myself into his lame-brain plan. Guilt will drive anyone to become a fool, and I was wracked with guilt: guilt over damning the legacy of my sweet mom, guilt over insulting the love of my father's life, and guilt over being the unworthy son of a father who was no good at parenting. Okay, Dad, I tell myself, there is a six-foot surf out there and very likely this old canoe will capsize. We may sink out there, but we can both swim and hopefully we will capsize while we are still in shallow water. And if by some miracle it leaks we won't get far. So let's do it. If we don't, my guilt will choke the life out of me anyway.

Close to the water is a tide line. It is full of seaweed, kelp and bits of dead wood and other debris. It is slippery. Dad's leg goes straight out and he topples. On the way down, he drops his side of the canoe, and it lands on a rock in the middle of the tide line. The canoe cracks. Doggone it. I volley between feeling lucky and feeling destined to live a life of guilt.

I put my side down carefully, though this is as stupid as trying to launch the boat since the canoe is already busted and care would not do any good now. Dad's left side is covered in thick black mud. He is still lying in the mud. I offer my hand. I'm still scared, so my hand is quivering. He looks at it, grabs it and pulls me down instead of helping himself up. As I slop about in the mud beside him, he pops a guffaw that leads him straight to hysterical laughter. It is contagious. I laugh too. We both laugh till we cry. Once the crying comes, it grows into the biggest cry I have ever experienced. We lean on Dad's granddad's broken canoe and cry over Mom's broken dream of reviving this old boat. We cry over not being a good dad or a good son, and finally we know we are both crying over our mutual loss. We stop only when we are too exhausted to shed another tear.

By the time we finish, the tide is tickling our feet. I look up at the sun shining down on us, and it dawns on me that I knew how to be a son to my mother but I do not know how to be a son to my father. I don't want to say anything bad about my mom, she was the most loving being in our lives, but she didn't do us any favours by fixing things between us: we never learned to get along without her. We have been around each other for fifteen years and yet neither of us has a clue how to enjoy being together. I lean my head into my dad's shoulder.

"Remember, you said you don't know how to parent a son?"

Dad flinches, then lets go a cautious, "Yeah," like he doesn't really want to have to pay for his honesty, his helplessness or his rage, but like a champ he is stepping up to the plate to take his medicine.

"Well, I really don't know how to be a son either. Mom's gone, so I can't be her son anymore. I have to learn to be yours."

"We're in a helluva fix then, aren't we?" And we laugh again. He jumps up and heads for the house. I'm not sure that the conversation was over, so I just stand there looking at his receding back. The water sneaks up and curls around my wet shoes before he turns.

"Well, first thing you have to know about being my son is that I don't stand around waiting for someone to serve up the next activity and you shouldn't either. The boat is busted and the tide is up, so that activity is over. We will learn to be father and son in the coming years as one activity leads us to the next." I follow him up the shore.

"What's next?"

"Supper," he drops flatly.

He peels off his wet clothes and I do too. I see the youthful swan trying to fly and nod in its direction. Dad and I stand half naked, dripping wet, and watch that swan take flight. The swan lacks elegance and strength at first. In near full flight, he weakens and comes crashing down toward the surf. His wings nearly succumb to the sea. I tense. I feel like that swan, graceless and not quite strong enough for manhood. "Fly boy, fly," I whisper, and by some miracle he finds the will and grace to flap his wings and raise himself up. I watch relieved. Maybe I could do this too.

"Supper sounds good," I say as I toss some cedar over the porch toward the swan. I thank the swan, my dad and my mom. Dad is holding the door open. As I enter, he touches my shoulder just barely. There is a new sweetness in the lightness of his touch. It feels so good. Inside, he pulls the last quart of fish my mom had canned a year ago from the shelf and hands me a paring knife.

"You peel the potatoes and I'll make salmon patties." We putter about the kitchen in silence for a while. I can't help chuckling quietly to myself about the picture we must have made as we rolled about in the mud. One chuckle reaches the air and I look over to Dad. His eyes smile brightly.

"We can make another," he says, stirring the fish hash he's frying.

"Canoe? You know how to do that?" I ask surprised.

"Nah, but it can't be that hard, an adze, a log and some fire is all we need."

I just stare at him. Is he nuts? No, he must be joking.

"Well, someone must have dreamed that first one into being." He was serious. Momma had dreams. Dad hadn't much cared to

dream with her when she was alive, but now he is picking up her bundle. I choke a little as I realize her dreams must have centered on me, and my dad is determined to realize them for her, one activity at a time.